GRUMPY OLD CHRISTMAS

'Tis the season to be Jolly – Grumpy...

In the case of the Grumpy Old Man 'tis the season to have to put up with even deeper layers of vexation than usual. From breakfast presenters who tell us it's now just 120 shopping days to go, to the annual festive strike by airport baggage handlers. From office parties to parents videoing their precocious brats at the atrocious school nativity play where your kid is playing the part of the donkey's rear end, and the 150th opportunity to see Whistle Down the Wind on the telly. Speaking of wind, there's the Xmas turkey that sends your digestive system to hell...

GRUMPY OLD CHRISTMAS

GRUMPY OLD CHRISTMAS

by

Stuart Prebble

Dales Large Print Books
Long Preston, North Yorkshire,
BD23 4ND, England.

British Library Cataloguing in Publication Data.

Prebble, Stuart
    Grumpy old Christmas.

A catalogue record of this book is
available from the British Library

ISBN   978-1-84262-695-5 pbk

First published in Great Britain in 2006
by Weidenfeld & Nicolson

Copyright © Stuart Prebble 2006

Cover illustration by arrangement with The Orion Publishing
Group

Published in Large Print 2009 by arrangement with
Orion Publishing Group

Dales Large Print is an imprint of Library Magna Books Ltd.

Printed and bound in Great Britain by
T.J. (International) Ltd., Cornwall, PL28 8RW

Contents

Preface

If you are a Grumpy Old Man, the chances are that you have been given this book as a Christmas present.

Indeed, the likelihood is that it's Christmas morning right now, and you've received this book about ten seconds ago. In fact, I've got a strong feeling that you have just opened the wrapping paper, and are having to flick through the first couple of pages with a half-smile on your face to show that you are appreciative and can't wait to get started on reading it. Yes, I've got a clear mental image of you squinting at the irritatingly tiny type and wondering where the hell your specs are.

Whoever has given it to you – most likely your impertinent kids or lovely wife or sister-in-law – is looking at your face right at this very moment for signs of your reactions. And if that's the case, you're probably wondering how on earth you're going to show something resembling appreciation, when you've already dug deep into your reserves of dissembling to indicate pleasure at receiving a de-luxe car-care kit, a novelty tie, a CD of Santana's greatest hits that you've already got, and a bottle of red wine with 'Old Git' written on the side.

Well, you've got a couple of alternatives (and I know I can't keep you long because you're going to have to react in the next few seconds or so). One of them is: 'Oh thanks so much. I've loved the TV series and this is by the same bloke who wrote it. I'll enjoy that.' That's got a lot to recommend it. It's polite, neutral and will allow you to move swiftly on to open the plastic wood-effect cuff-link tidy that goes next to your bed. (Good luck with showing appreciation for that one, by the way.)

Another is to tell the truth, which is more along the lines of: 'If one more person reminds me this year that I'm just like all those miserable bastards on the telly because I'm always going on and on about the same things they are going on about, I'll drill out their brain and fill the hole with snow.' Maybe that one is less warmly to be recommended; it may be seasonal, but perhaps it doesn't get Christmas off to quite the start you all want.

So how about a response which just gives everyone a good laugh because it confirms for them that you are, as they all already suspect, a Grumpy Old Man who can just about tolerate all the bollocks surrounding

Christmas, but is unlikely to want to throw a party every time someone gives you a modestly amusing gift.

Something like: 'Mmm. Thanks. Just what I wanted.'

That'll give them all a little anecdote to tell about you to their friends. 'Yeah, the old man just about raised a smile when we gave him that book about the bloody stupid TV series. Yeah, right, proves he's a grumpy old bastard. Pass the alco-pops.'

OK? So, repeat after me, with feeling: 'Mmm. Thanks. Just what I wanted.'

Congratulations. You've just given purpose to our lives as Grumpies – for it is our lot to spread a little innocent amusement at our own expense to those around us, and I can almost hear the gales of laughter echoing across time and space.

And the book? Well, my advice would be to put it in the bog and read a paragraph or two when you are taking a shit. That's more or less how I wrote it. But don't worry; I always remembered to wash my hands.

SP

1

'Tis the Season to be Grumpy

So ... I've been trying to think what it is. You know, what it is in particular about Christmas that brings out the worst in Grumpy Old Men. Why should it be, do you suppose, that while everyone else is wishing each other a merry Christmas, sending festive greetings cards to people they scarcely see from one year to the next, thinking about goodwill to all men, why is it that this is the time of year most guaranteed to get up our snitches?

Well, I guess you can take your pick really, can't you? It's anything and everything – from the breakfast telly presenters who tell us there are now just 120 shopping days to go, to the annual festive strike by airport baggage handlers.

From office parties where drunken juniors, who have waited the whole year for the opportunity, finally tell you what 'the trouble with you is...', to parents videoing their precocious brats starring in the atrocious school nativity play when your kid is playing the part of the donkey's rear end.

From the woman next door who drops in to show your wife the diamond ring her prat of a husband has bought her, to the 150th opportunity to see *Whistle Down the Wind* on the telly.

From that very special variety of constipation you feel after eating more turkey in one meal than you eat in the whole of the rest of the year put together, to the unvarnished joy of picking Christmas tree needles out of the fibres of your car rugs right up to Easter.

Oh yes, it's all this and so very much more.

But none of that quite captures the essence of it. Sure, there is irritation in all of the above and so much more besides, but as far as the average Grumpy Old Man is concerned, it's all much of a muchness. All just variations on the general theme. None of these events on their own, nor even the whole collection, quite accounts for the very particular brand of crabby grouchiness that pervades us at this time of the year.

Well, the good news is that I think I have the answer. I've given it an enormous amount of thought; far more, in fact, than is good for me or for those unfortunate enough to be around me. But I've got it. And now I'm going to share it with you.

Ready?

The main reason why we are at our grouchiest, grumpiest, uncontrollably mitherly worst at this time of year is that "'tis the season to be jolly'. Yes that's right, you know the sort of thing. 'Deck the halls with whatever it is of holly...' "'Tis the season to be jolly. Tra la la la la la la la la.'

Now exactly why on earth would that be? Why would this be the season to be jolly? What the hell has any of us got to be jolly about? Does anyone have any idea?

Let's face it. It's been yet another crap year, and the only thing that feels remotely worth celebrating is that, in spite of everything and to the disappointment of many of the people close to you, it looks as though you might be surviving to the end of it. Everything is worse. Yes, I mean that; everything.

I repeat the 'everything' because you may think I'm joking. Why should I say that? Well, because I've found that since I've been writing these books and TV series about the lives and loathes of Grumpy Old Men, quite a few people seem to feel the need to have a little laugh about it.

'Oh we love that series,' they'll often say. 'We agree with every word of it.' All of which is nice, and even I am not so grumpy that I don't enjoy the occasional compliment. But then they'll go ahead and spoil it. 'Of course, you're joking, right? Obviously it's not really true that most things are worse, is it?'

Usually at this point they look at me, half hopefully, as though I'm going to say something like: 'Oh yes, of course most things are better, but it's just that I think it's a jolly jape to run around the place saying that everything is worse.' As though I'm just doing it for some sort of perverse pleasure or for the sake of my health. Yes, that's right; I jaunt around *thinking* that everything is getting so much better, but *saying* that everything is getting so much worse. For fun.

So let's be clear. I mean it. I'm not trying to be funny (which may be just as well, I hear you say). This year everything has got so much worse. I mean everything.

Don't believe me? Well, let's go through a few things, shall we? Let's start with the personal as it applies to me, but as it may also apply, at least in part, to you.

Another year has all but passed and I'm a little bit older. A little bit fatter. A little bit greyer. A little bit thinner on top, but I have a little bit more hair growing out of my ears and nose. I'm a little bit more wrinkly and a little bit stiffer in the joints. I sleep a little bit less well, my digestion plays up just a little bit more, I've got a little bit less money and my car is a little bit closer to needing to be replaced. My endowment mortgage is promising to disappoint, the PEP I was advised to start ten years ago still hasn't returned to the value it had in 1996, and the lovely Gordon

16

has just told me that I'll probably have to work to sixty-eight if I want a pension.

My house is in a little bit worse state of repair and the decorator is a little bit less likely to come since I told him last time that Stephen Hawking could have done a better job of wallpapering the hallway. My children are just a little bit more costly and a little bit more objectionable. My wife is just a little bit more irritated with me and one of the cats has died.

Why has the cat dying made my year worse, considering that I don't like cats? That's easy; we've still got one cat left and somehow or other, inexplicably, one cat seems more of a bloody nuisance than two.

OK, OK, a little self-centred. A little ego-centric. That's just me. What about the rest of you? Even if everything is getting worse for me personally, surely it isn't doing so in the wider world? OK, where should we start? It doesn't matter; we can start anywhere.

Every time I pick up the newspapers, even the proper ones, I'm reading on page one about the impending marriage/pregnancy/divorce of celebrity airhead number one to airhead number two, while I have to wait till about page twelve to read a story about anything that actually matters. Every time I turn on the telly the news presenters are behaving as though they are my 'mate' in some way and are addressing me as though we're in a pub. Every time I turn on the radio there is some totally gibbering idiot warbling mindless vacuous rubbish in between bits and pieces of what passes for music but which is actually totally disposable bollocks that is hardly even here today before it's gone tomorrow.

There is a little bit more traffic and most of the owners of all those extra cars must live and work near me because my commute takes a little bit longer. (Sorry, that's about me again, but it could just as easily be about you.) There's a few more people who want to dig up the road, and the people who want to dig up the road are even less likely than they once were to call each other up and ask if there's anything anyone else wants to do beneath the surface while they're at it. There's a few more people putting obelisks in the road, further obstructing a journey to work which is already like a bloody commando assault course.

The price of anything I want to buy is just a little bit higher, and is now about five times what I think would be reasonable rather than four times as it was last year. There is just a bit more crime, and a bit more of whatever crime there is seems to be violent crime. The police seem less likely to catch anyone for anything as trivial as breaking into someone else's house, and when they do, a judge ticks them off. Despite that, the prisons are full and we have to build more if there is not to be a 'crisis'.

Oh, and there is, of course, a 'crisis' in the health service.

Enough already? We have hardly even started.

There is just a little bit more tension in the world and on any given day any of us seems just a little bit more likely to get blown to smithereens for some cause that we won't even get a glimpse of as our brains are flying in one direction and our feet in another. There's just a little bit more racial tension, just a little bit bigger gap between rich and poor, and we're just a little bit closer to whichever is the version of Far Eastern flu that's eventually going to wipe out the majority of us. The education system is worse, vandalism is worse, politicians are worse. Oh, and at this time of the year it's getting colder. And wetter.

So, fairly shit, huh? Not much to celebrate there, do you think? But oddly enough, none of that is really the problem. Grumpy Old Men aren't especially grumpy because everything has become worse. Good God, we're well used to that by now, or at least we should be. No, Grumpy Old Men are grumpy at this time of the year because, despite all of the above and so much more, ''Tis the season to be jolly', and so everyone around us is trying so very hard to be so.

Which would be bad enough if they just got on with trying to 'be jolly' and left us the hell alone. But they don't. It even somehow seems to be a constituent part of their jolliness, for some reason we can only guess at, that we should also 'be jolly' with them. (Some hope!)

They say things to us like: 'Cheer up, it might never happen' – which is a complete misunderstanding. We're not looking glum because we're expecting anything bad to happen; not dreading anything. We're just grumpy because of what is. Because of the human condition. Because the world is so screwed up that being grumpy is the only rational thing to be. And being surrounded by people imbued with a seasonally adjusted sense of bubbly bonhomie is not going to contribute a feline fart to cheering us up. Quite the contrary. We're grumpy in any event, and we're grumpier than ordinarily we would be because cheerful people around us are saying things like: 'Cheer up, it'll soon be Christmas.'

As if.

So that's it then. If you are someone who wants to deck the halls with thingummys of holly, that's great for you. Enjoy it. But if you've got a Grumpy Old Man in your life, your best Christmas gift to him would be to leave him the hell alone.

Or does that seem a bit too grumpy?

2

On the First Day of Christmas...

Last year it happened on 10 October. What happened? The beginning of the nightmare before Christmas, that's what. The nightmare that lasts from the first moment someone mentions Christmas, right up to Christmas itself and beyond.

Last summer I made a mental note to make a mental note of the first moment when someone pointed out how many, or rather how few, shopping days there were till Christmas.

It happened on 10 October and it was on breakfast telly; but I'm not going to say which channel because I'm in danger of being unfair to my friends on GMTV whose morning programmes I watch most days. It seems a bit harsh that I choose to watch them because I prefer their programmes, and then spend the whole time rambling on about everything they do that irritates me.

Therefore let's just say it was on breakfast telly, and not say which channel. So it was on 10 October that Penny (we're going to call her Penny even though that isn't her real name) pointed out that there were now just seventy-one shopping days or whatever until Christmas. I'm not quite sure why or what the story was – something about predictions from retailers of a shortage of myrrh, or whatever.

Anyhow, until that moment I hadn't seen a single TV advertisement, nor a single festive decoration in the shops. No sign of anything untoward. Life was as normal as it ever can be for a Grumpy. But then it was almost as though everyone else had been waiting for that first mention as a kind of starting-pistol; one person had said the dreaded word and the floodgates opened. Because from that day onwards, everywhere I looked, I saw references to Christmas.

TV ads for toys competing to be the 'must-have' children's gift this Christmas. Newspaper ads from the Royal Mail telling us the last posting day if you want to send a card to your Auntie Rosemary in Papua New Guinea. Every nitwit columnist in every newspaper or magazine seems to think it's necessary to tell us about their little Christmas dilemma, like we could possibly care. The news is full of supposed alarm at whichever essential service is going on strike. Whose turn is it this year? Air traffic controllers? Baggage handlers? Train drivers? Gravediggers? All of the above?

And then it starts in the shops. The first

signs are the little displays in corners of department stores that seem somehow embarrassed by their own presence. Probably it's a counter displaying a heavily discounted set of gaudy baubles which are obviously left over from last year. Maybe a couple of Christmas puddings will begin to appear on the lower shelves of the supermarkets, awaiting elevation. Brandy butter, mince pies, and gradually they'll spread like a rash upwards and across the display. It's like an icebreaker, and everyone walking past is shaking their heads muttering, 'It gets earlier every year' and other familiar refrains

Then, with the same certainty and regularity as the first cuckoo in spring or the avalanche of utility bills in January, it's not long before the first lists start appearing.

We have quite a long kitchen table in our house, and one end is more or less permanently made over to the bureaucratic aspects of my wife's apparently rather complicated life. It's a small clutter of letters to and from friends in Australia, birthday cards, get well cards, anniversary cards, house-warming cards, congratulations cards, sympathy cards, thank you cards, and an assortment of little cards that have been handpainted and have scraps of leftover lace or sequins attached to them just in case she needs to write a short note to someone on a subject not covered by the collection of generic cards above.

Then there will be the odd catalogue – featuring assorted clothes, shoes, household goods etc. – an occasional holiday brochure, a copy of *Good Housekeeping* from last April, a collection of receipts for things that may or may not be going back to the shops, address book, calendar... I hope by now you're getting the idea.

Among all this debris there are usually two or three handwritten lists. These I usually regard as nothing to do with me, so I barely ever glance at them. But if I do, I'm always immediately at a loss to work out how some subjects got onto one list, and how other subjects got onto another. One will typically say things like 'cat's inoculations', 'Miren's birthday' and 'Trinny and Susannah, 8 p.m.' Another will be full of things like 'book holidays', 'get house valued' and 'Marmite'. I know, I know; who would dare to try to penetrate or comprehend the mind that lumps these things together?

The point is that one of the early signals that Christmas has already appeared over the distant horizon and is galloping fast in our direction with all the promise of a scene from *Zulu* is a radical change in the contents of all these lists. From early November onwards there are far fewer 'brochures for Barcelona' or reminders to try a new recipe from Nigella, and much more of 'curtains to dry cleaners', 'shampoo bedroom carpet' and 'decorate downstairs loo'. Like Santa is not so busy on the night before Christmas that he's going to take a quick tour of the house to ensure that the bedrooms are spic and span, and maybe will take a quick slash in the downstairs john.

But the first sign of Christmas getting under way, in our household at least, is the annual festive appearance of the Christmas card list. This is an immediately recognisable document because it seems to be only about five minutes since it was last making itself felt as a constant presence on the kitchen worktop near to the telephone.

Ordinarily I make it my business to avoid even glancing at a document like this, because it also clearly comes under the category of 'nothing to do with me' and of course I would very much prefer that it should remain that way. However, I can't help but notice that my wife has developed rather an elaborate code, which seems to group people into a number of categories.

At the top, their names written in clear and bold handwriting indicating total absence of doubt, are the people who are definitely going to get a Christmas card from us. Mum, Malcolm and Kath, Steve and Helen, Peter and Nicky, Andy and Tina, Di and Ian, John and Yvonne, etc., etc. I reckon there are about sixty people or couples on this list.

This is the category of people we see and/

or speak to on a very regular basis during the course of the year, and who therefore don't in my view need to be reminded by receiving a Christmas card from us that we're still alive. They also don't need to know – because we're close friends or relatives and they can pretty much take it for granted – that we wish them a merry Christmas, or whatever it is. I have on one or two occasions pointed out the absurdity, therefore, of sending a Christmas card to these people, but it has turned out not to be an area which is open to debate. If you are in this category, you're going to get a Christmas card from us, and that's that.

The next group – their names written in handwriting which might be a little less determined, as though to suggest that a bit of thought has gone on in between each name – consists of the people we don't see or speak to from one year to the next. These people are also unlikely to imagine that we don't wish them appropriate season's greetings, but for some reason do apparently need to be reminded at Christmas that we are still alive. This list includes various aunts and uncles, to some of whom we are so close that I have never met them. Pen-pal relatives. There are one or two of my wife's old friends from school, some of whom she hasn't met for forty years. There are some neighbours who used to live next door to us at houses we haven't lived in for twenty years and who, if they are still alive, probably don't still live next door. Even one or two couples we met on holidays several lifetimes ago. These people are also undoubtedly going to have their festive season immeasurably enriched by receiving a card from us. It won't say 'Happy Christmas – we're still breathing', but that's what it ought to say.

Then there is a third group. This one we should call the 'I really don't think we will send them a card this year – unless of course we receive one from them' list. Quite a few people on this list have already disqualified themselves from receiving a card from us this year, because the absence of a little cross next to their names indicates that we didn't receive a card from them last year. So they may either be dead or perhaps are thinking the same thing about us that we are thinking about them. In the case of all these people, it seems that we'll wait until a card from them drops through the letter-box, say, 'Oh bugger, we've received a card from Jim and Rosemary' and then send them one.

This only works, of course, if we receive the card before about 23 December. To post one after that indicates without doubt that the card has been an after-thought.

However, the fact that they've sent us a card this year means that they'll probably have to go back on the list for next year;

meanwhile, the fact that they haven't received a card from us this year may well mean that we're off their Christmas card list for next year, and so it will go on – alternating until one of us dies or all of us come to our senses.

(It's probably worth adding that if you receive a card from us posted after about the 22nd, with a handwritten PS inside saying something like, 'Oh to be better organised', you can pretty well guess that we were not going to send you a card until we received the one from you.)

Next on the list is a category of people who will receive a card from us, but the card is not the point. They are on the list because it's a reminder to ourselves that this is a good time to give a small gratuity to the various people to whom we are in one way or another in thrall for the rest of the year. This includes, of course, the dustmen so that they will kindly continue for another twelve months to take away all the various items which they could, at their own discretion, easily leave for us to cart to the local tip. Stuff like bags of leaves or the odd out-of-date computer monitor. It includes our regular postman who, unlike his various colleagues who take over from him on his days or weeks off seems to be able to read. It includes the bloke who delivers our newspaper because he is kind enough to do so before lunch on most days, and until fairly recently it used to include the milkman, before he became an object of nostalgia.

A week or two after the appearance of the Christmas card list, the actual Christmas cards we are going to send will start to appear, again in various batches. (I say 'we' but, of course, I don't mean 'we', as we'll see later.)

I'm not quite sure why we don't send the same Christmas card to everyone, and the allocation of particular cards to particular people is an art-form far too subtle for me or any other self-respecting Grumpy to comprehend. It's something along the lines of 'She's arty so I thought she'd appreciate that one' – which I have to admit leaves me totally at a loss for comment.

Sometimes, Christmas cards come in packs of one kind or another, but in order to buy the ones you want, you also have to buy a whole load more with pictures of snowmen in scarves and with carrots for noses or whatever. If you get a picture of a snowman in a scarf from us, you can probably reckon you're on the C list.

You must have wondered, as I have, why it is that Christmas cards in general are so uniformly uninspiring: a picture of a robin – a nasty and vicious bird with no obvious connection with Christmas; a golden bell which has been slightly raised from the front of the card; a Victorian street-scene with snow. They all leave me cold. And while not especially sentimental about Christmas, I am assuredly not a fan of the rude or otherwise distasteful Christmas card – you know the sort of thing – risqué jokes about what might be going on between Mum and Santa under the mistletoe. Tortured cartoons about roasting nuts. Oh dear.

To add still further to the complexities, my wife has one or two favourite charities, and seems to think that Christmas is a good time to give them some extra money by buying their greetings cards. The trouble is that very often the charity she wants to support has a rather horrible selection of cards. So we have a dilemma: send crap Christmas cards that indicate that we are nice people, or cards with a nicer picture on the front that benefit no one but the manufacturer.

See? It's a tricky business, this Christmas card-sending lark. You probably thought it was simple, but it's the sort of thing that can plague us Grumpies. And all that's bad enough – can you imagine how much worse it would be if we actually sent any ourselves?

Being a Grumpy obviously means that I don't send any Christmas cards at all. Haven't done for years. However, there is a last category on the long list described above, with a very few names on it, whom my wife describes as 'my friends'. I'm not sure quite how they got to be in the category of 'my friends' rather than 'our friends' – probably because they are in some way related to work – but anyway, a couple of weeks before Christmas we have a little ritual in which I'm asked if I want to send them a card this year.

My problem is that the answer very much depends on what particular mood I'm in at the moment I'm being asked. I've found in recent years that I'm just as likely to say 'no way' to all of them, as I am to respond indignantly that, of course, we should send a card to them – aren't we sending cards to all 'your friends'? So the result is that some years 'my friends' will receive a card from us, and some years they won't. Maybe they wonder about that, but I suspect that, much like myself, they don't even notice.

I say that I don't send any cards, but I actually send hundreds – from the office. Every year we have our own card printed – recently featuring, as you might imagine, a selection of the Grumpy Old Men from the series, and everyone in the office signs their first name on about 200 of them. Some poor sod then gets the job of typing names and addresses on envelopes and popping them in the post to the 200 or so people who've worked with us or for us, or for whom we've worked, in the last twelve months.

How thrilled are these people, do you suppose, to receive an impersonal card from us, signed by about twenty names, only a couple of which they will recognise? Well, my guess is that they are every bit as thrilled as I am when I receive the equivalent from them; that is to say, the cards are greeted with something between indifference and irritation. What the hell – not to put too fine a point on it – could possibly be the point of that? Unless it is to remind them that Christmas is an excellent time for giving us some extra business.

I pause momentarily to say that, believe it or not, at one time I myself was *un très grand fromage* in ITV, in a position to give business to a lot of TV producers and others. Oddly enough, my jokes were never so funny before or since, my ideas were never better received, and boy did I receive a lot of Christmas cards. Funnily enough, I don't seem to get quite so many now though. Weird, huh?

Anyway, back at home, my wife is going to allocate what seems like all the evenings in December to writing Christmas cards. Again, having signed 200 of them at work in about half an hour, I cannot for the life of me work out how on earth this process can take so long, but needless to say I have not enquired. The terror involved in the likely response of 'well, why don't you do it then?' rules out any such enquiry.

However, I have noticed that many of the cards she sends will contain an appropriate phrase or two alongside the conventional greeting. As it's the only time in the year that she's going to communicate with her friend Julie with whom she went to school the best part of forty years ago, it seems to her appropriate to write something more than 'merry Christmas', so Julie will get a couple of sentences.

As this is nothing to do with me, I can't really be grumpy about it. At least my wife is tailoring her message to the person to whom she is writing. We have not, thank heavens, succumbed to the round robin, which I believe must have been imported from the New World and seems increasingly favoured among our friends.

Wouldn't it be wonderful, don't you think, to receive a round robin letter at Christmas from someone whose children hadn't passed all their exams with flying colours, who hadn't just recently had another promotion, who hadn't bought themselves the new BMW or taken their holidays in St Kitts? Wouldn't it be great to get one that said: 'Another crap year, we're getting divorced, the kids are all unemployed, on drugs, have turned out to be cross-dressers and have tattoos.' But somehow, we don't ever seem to get any of those.

(Actually I pause here to remark that we used to receive regular bulletins of the round robin type from one or two families we rather like – until I said something disparag-

33

ing about the practice in our BBC2 programme about Christmas. Since then, we've stopped receiving them – though whether this means that they've stopped altogether, or it's just that we are now deemed to be too grumpy to be allowed to receive them, one can only speculate. Anyway, if any of our friends who used to send us round robins are reading this, my wife misses them even if I don't, so please resume.)

At this point, I was also going to go into a little capsule of bile about people who send you a Christmas card featuring a photograph of their wonderful family, or their house, or their house in the country or whatever – but my wife has pointed out that one or two people whom we really quite like do that, so I've got to desist. Pity – but I feel that I've already provided the template – you can fill in the colours yourselves.

Of course the other great joy about Christmas cards is the one you receive from 'George and Rose' and you have no idea who George and Rose are. In the *Christmas Grumpy Old Men* Special on BBC, John O'Farrell speculated that

There's a bloke somewhere in this country with a very perverse sense of humour, who sits at home sending everybody Christmas cards from made-up couples. So every year you open your Christmas card and you go, 'Happy Christmas

from Roy and Jane.' And you go, 'Roy and Jane? Who are Roy and Jane? These must be friends of yours from work, darling.' 'No, I don't know Roy and Jane. They're not that couple we met on holiday, are they?' 'No, is that, actually is that Jane or is that James? Do you know a gay couple called Roy and James?'

And I think you'll agree that he's right.

There is another fairly recent development on the subject of Christmas greetings which cannot be allowed to pass without a little gripe, and that is the advent of the electronic Christmas card. Obviously I'm not going to be able to write as an expert on this subject, because though I have received plenty of them, I have never actually opened one. To me, or any other Grumpy Old Man, the notion that someone is going to e-mail us what I believe is called a hyperlink, and we're going to go to the trouble of clicking it, waiting for it to upload, or download or whatever, so that it can show us a ridiculous or offensive cartoon to the tune of 'Jingle Bells', is indeed far-fetched. We're never going to open them. We're always going to delete them as soon as we know what they are. Don't bother to send them to Grumpies.

Though I'm against Christmas in general and Christmas cards in particular, at least the act of sending a Christmas card involves going out, buying the card, writing a greeting, buying a stamp, writing the address and posting the envelope. If all you can be bothered to do is to send the same electronic message to everyone in your address book, it's my strong feeling that you're best off not bothering. Really.

And then, of course, there is the confluence of two relatively recent phenomena – electronic cards and formalised charity-giving at Christmas. This introduces a whole new area to be grumpy about. What about the electronic Christmas card which says that, instead of sending you a Christmas card through the post, the sender has made a donation to charity? What effect does this have on you?

If you're anything like me, the only question I want an answer to is 'How much?' Yes, that's right; how much did you give to charity? Did you carefully calculate how much you would otherwise have spent on buying and sending Christmas cards, deduct whatever was the cost of the electronic card, and give the balance to charity? Or did you save yourself a lot of time and effort and £150, but just give away £25 of it to charity?

There are not many opportunities in life to seem like an altruistic person and save money at the same time. If you have taken this one, I think we should be told.

And here's the one that caps the lot. This year, for the first time, we received through the post a pre-printed but otherwise blank card from a family we know and rather like, which said that they were not sending Christmas cards, but were instead making a donation to the Pakistan Earthquake appeal. So what are you going to make of that? They've gone to very nearly the entire trouble and expense of sending a Christmas card to everyone they know, just to tell them that they're not sending a Christmas card but instead giving the money to charity. Is that wild, or what?

So here's the official Grumpy Old Man philosophy about Christmas cards. Those who know you and like you probably know that you wish them to have a happy Christmas, as indeed you wish them well all the rest of the year. They don't need to receive a card.

Those to whom you haven't spoken for twelve months, don't give a bugger about you and frankly you don't give a bugger about them, so what's the point? They don't need to receive a card either. Business contacts should all stop sending cards to each other – it's a total waste of time, effort and money, all of which could be better spent on something creative. And lastly, here's the thing about giving to charity (and since this is a festival about Jesus, let me refer you to the parable of the Widow's Mite). If you want to make a donation to charity, the thing to do is to make the donation, and shut the fuck up about it.

A bit harsh? I know. Christmas is coming, so maybe I should try to be a bit nicer...

3

The Good Old Days

One of the many ways that we Grumpy Old Men find to bore everyone else to death is to talk fondly and endlessly about the 'good old days', and by that, of course, we mean the period of our formative years; the sixties and seventies when we all grew our hair over our ears and collars, starting doing inverted V signs everywhere we went, and thought the world was becoming a better place.

However, what I find we talk about less are the 'good old days' before that, in the fifties, when we were kids. Because for most of us, if we're honest, those particular 'good old days' weren't so good at all. The truth is that, for everyone I know, the most vivid feature of the 'good old days' in the fifties was what in these modern times we would think of as more or less grinding poverty.

Our old man had two jobs and our mother worked part-time, and they just about rubbed along well enough to provide essentials, putting a few florins in a row of jam jars for the electricity, the gas, and for clothes. All through the year they used to save spare sixpences in a 'Dimple' whisky bottle, which they would break open in the few days coming up to our annual holidays. I believe that the contents might amount to £16 or so.

It's a cliché now and no one believes you, but we would have a small joint (of meat) for what we called dinner at Sunday lunchtime, and whatever was left over would re-emerge in various guises at least until Wednesday. Shepherds' pie, bubble and squeak and so on. These were the days before batteries (not that kind), and chicken was an almost unheard-of luxury treat.

Weekdays we used to have a mid-day meal of overcooked slop at school, and most evenings we'd have toast and dripping for our tea. My mother used to send us to the corner shop to get groceries, and we would hand over her purse to Mrs Corbin who could be trusted to take out elevenpence-halfpenny for a loaf of sliced white. We always hoped it would be Mrs Corbin because Mr Corbin had had what later on in life I learned was a stroke, and walked very slowly and dribbled. I can remember my mother weeping as she realised that she wasn't going to be able to pay the rent-man on Friday.

Like most women at the time, other than the well-to-do, my mother's life when we

39

were growing up was one of more or less relentless drudgery. Everyday chores which we now carry out with the press of a few overcomplicated buttons, in those days constituted a whole week of work. How did it go? Monday washing day, Tuesday drying day, Wednesday ironing day, Thursday airing day, Friday the old man wears it to go out to the pub, comes back pissed and wants a shag or a fight. Neither of which, I'm guessing, was especially welcome. (Actually, I have to be fair to my parents because they are looking over my shoulder from heaven as I write. Therefore I am compelled to admit that this latter part didn't happen in our house because my mother more or less ran things; but all the rest did.)

The kids next door had rickets, those on the other side had nits, and you were the posh cissy on the estate if your old man had a car.

Yes, despite what I said before about grinding poverty, our old man had a car. Actually, he had a series of cars. Like everyone else, we used to call them 'old bangers'. He had to park the car on a hill at the side of the flats so he could bump-start it in the mornings, and used to put bricks in front of the tyres to stop it from rolling down the hill because the brakes were unreliable. I call them tyres, but they were flat and smooth and you could see glimpses of the canvas that held them together where the tread was supposed to be.

My dad used to spend the greater part of most weekends lying on the pavement underneath the cars – Austin A35s or A47s, Morris Oxfords and eventually a super-duper Vauxhall Victor in two tones of green – in a continuous but ultimately doomed battle with corroding exhausts, or sumps, or big ends or something. Large oil stains on the side of the road marked his parking place.

Now you may be wondering what is the purpose and relevance of this no doubt gripping trip down Benton's lane? Well, the point is that the 'good old days' were not very good in several respects. But one of the many many reasons why Grumpy Old Men are especially grumpy at Christmas is that Christmas can never again be as good as it was when we were kids. And that's because we had nothing, and the thrill and excitement of receiving *anything* when you've got *nothing* is a thrill beyond dreams.

I'm not saying that 'kids have too much these days'. Even Grumpy Old Men grew up hearing that – from granddads who had fought in the trenches and grandmas worn out from their daily struggle with the mangle. Actually, what I've come to realise is that every generation gives their kids whatever they can afford to give them at Christmas – no matter how rich or poor they are.

Think about it. Your grandparents used to

get an orange and a whip and top for Christmas and were told to be grateful for them or get a clip round the ear; but they didn't need to be told because for them a piece of citrus fruit and a piece of domination equipment were the contemporary equivalent to an all-expenses trip to the Bahamas.

With kids today it's a struggle to think of anything to buy them for Christmas that they haven't already got, or probably would be getting at some point soon in the general course of things. And ultimately the downside of all the relative prosperity which, thank God, most of us now currently enjoy is that you can't ever relive the days when you had bloody nothing, and so getting bloody anything was an enormous treat.

Nothing is as thrilling, or can be, as the hula hoop or compendium of games were when they were by far and away the most exciting thing that was going to happen to you that year. You remember – a crappy old draughts board made out of cardboard and a little plastic egg-cup thingy to rattle two dice in before throwing them.

Nothing comes close. Snorkelling among the tropical fish in the Maldives is great, but doesn't get off the starting blocks in comparison to that feeling of bursting into the living room as an eight-year-old in darned pyjamas and seeing a pile of packages wrapped up and with your name on them. A really nice meal in an inexpensive restaurant can be enjoyable, but doesn't register on the same Richter scale as ripping open the paper and finding a Meccano set. And nothing, and I do mean nothing, that anyone can buy a Grumpy Old Man in his thirties, forties, fifties or sixties is going to compare with his first two-wheeled bike. These were the thrills of a lifetime, and they aren't ever coming back as exquisitely and vividly again.

Do you remember much about Christmas when you were a kid? I do. It was beyond fabulous. Yes, we had a bit of a hard time for most of the year, but you have to hand it to them, my folks pushed the boat out when Christmas was coming. We didn't have two halfpennies to rub together (an odd expression I've always thought; why would one rub two halfpennies together? For warmth?), and for most of the year we were going to have to do without this and without that, but come Christmas they were going to do it right if it killed them.

Actually it's a working-class thing, this. These days we all sit there on the settee appalled by the news features about less well-off people running up huge debts because they're ordering from the catalogue stuff they can't afford, but it's the same thing now as then. How often have you heard it? 'We don't have a lot of money, but my Duane isn't going to go short at Christmas.'

Duane's mates are going to have the new designer trainers/PlayStation/video game/skateboard or whatever, and even if Mum has to spend the rest of the year paying for it at £5 a week, he is too. We can't see the difference between the pair of trainers you pay £15 for in Tesco and the pair of trainers you pay £115 in Nike or whatever – but the kids can see the difference, and their mates can see the difference, and that's what matters.

Only toffs have sufficient self-confidence to buy their stuff from the charity shop.

So anyway, back to the 1950s. I think that in those days, anticipation of Christmas started about the first week in December and grew to a frenzy. We didn't have Advent calendars, but boy did we know how many days it was till Christmas.

As kids, my brother and I were not encouraged to write Christmas lists, because even then we somehow knew that being acquisitive was unappealing. However, one way or another, we did make it known that our lives would be complete if somehow or other my parents could find a way to getting us a train set.

I don't know how on earth we could have imagined that such a thing might be possible. Perhaps it was because we didn't actually know that we were hard up because everyone around us was hard up too, and we didn't have a load of programmes on the telly specifically designed to tell us that money and happiness were the same thing. Advertisements were for things like Gibbs SR, or Omo – not so much for PlayStations or holidays in the Caribbean.

However, we did know enough to realise that something like a train set was likely to be well out of our reach. So being pragmatists, well before we knew what the word meant, we had let it be known that a train set would be almost unimaginably fantastic, but failing that, we'd be very happy indeed with something called a 'Soccerado'. This was, I believe, one of those little perspex boards on legs with a football pitch painted on the top. There were two teams of plastic men, one dressed in blue, one in red, each player with a small magnet at the base. Then there were four little rods with another magnet on the end, which you placed against the bottom surface of the board to manipulate your player around the pitch. You remember. Soccerado. Anyway, you get the idea.

So, Soccerado or a train set. Naturally, we'd prefer a train set, but Christmas would still be beyond wonderful if we just got a Soccerado.

The excitement of Christmas for us young boys grew in intensity over the weeks, and then days, before the big day itself, so that by the time Christmas Eve came around, we were practically erupting.

My brother and I shared a bedroom as kids, and we used to be determined to stay awake to catch Santa (when we were younger) or Dad (when we grew more cynical) delivering the presents. We would reinforce our efforts by taking it in turns to talk to the other one in order to stay awake. Never in my life, before or since, has time ticked by more slowly.

'What time is it now?' one of us might say, just about four minutes after the last time someone asked.

'A quarter past eleven.'

Well, a quarter past eleven was far later than either of us had ever stayed awake before. Merely to have our eyes open at such a forbidden time was an unrivalled excitement, but by then we were both struggling. I remember constructing little dramas in my head involving the cowboys and Indians that were scattered in various poses across the wallpaper. Playing cowboys and Indians was our favourite game in those days – always arguing about who got to circle the wagons and shoot the Winchesters, and who got to whoop and holler but ultimately to fall off his galloping bike and die a spectacular death.

We talked about our latest go-karts – made out of wooden boxes we had half-inched from the back of the greengrocer's shop and the wheels we acquired from prams (and now I have a strong image of an old-fashioned

46

pram with the wheels missing, propped up on bricks). We discussed how we might streamline our kart so it would go faster than the one being built by the Bradley kids, who both, I think, eventually went to prison for TDA. I don't remember dropping off to sleep, but I do remember waking at about four o'clock, it being pitch dark outside, and discussing with my brother whether it was too early to go and wake up our parents.

Several times we would be ushered back to bed and told 'Another two hours' which ticked by even more slowly than the longest minutes and seconds I was talking about from the previous night. One of us might drop off to sleep, only to be awoken again by the other, in paroxysms of anticipation. (Of course, we were too young and too working class in those days to know that it was called anticipation. Or that they were 'paroxysms'. In those days, we were just more or less wetting ourselves.)

Eventually, after a delay of about the same length as the second Ice Age, we heard signs of life from our parents; little bits of shuffling around. Had he been? Had he been? Had we been well-enough behaved these last weeks after all? Well no – we had been seen smashing glass milk bottles (remember them?) to smithereens with our catapults, and the old git from up the road had come down to tell our dad – but it seemed possible that he might have forgiven us.

At last we were allowed to walk down the hallway towards the living-room door, both parents gamely behaving as though they were every bit as unsure as we were about whether any of our wishes might have been fulfilled. My brother was (and is) older than me, and bigger too, so care had to be taken that the vista about to be unveiled to us was revealed to both at exactly the same moment. We stood side by side as the door opened – a little way – just enough to see that the room was still in near-pitch darkness, but that there were signs of a few small lights and movement. And that sound? Could that possibly be the sound of small electric motors running?

Finally the door was thrown open and there, I swear it, taking up at least a quarter of the total floor space of the room, was a train set – with two engines already pulling passenger and goods coaches around the tracks. If I had died and gone to heaven at that moment, it would have been worth it. I do not remember being that excited by anything until the birth of my first-born, and if I'm really honest, maybe not even then.

It was all mounted on a green board and I can see it as clearly now, forty-six years later, as I could then. There was an outer circle of track, with two sets of points enabling the train to change direction by moving diagonally across the layout, and there was another set of points which allowed a train to go into a siding which – thrill of thrills – was then raised in a sort of overpass above the existing track and all the way round the board to the other side, where there was a set of buffers. Three of the sets of points were electrically operated by little levers, and three more were manual. There were little lights here and there to illuminate the thing during the many hours to come of operating the system in darkness and, right across the middle, there was a little road system which intersected at a manually operated level-crossing. On the painted-on roads there were little cars, and there was a little garage with petrol pumps, little people, little trees and little post-boxes. In short, this train set incorporated every bit of the variety of attractions of modern-day Las Vegas, but without the surplus-to-requirements dancing girls.

And do you know what? After we had nearly fainted with excitement, and had played with the thing until the air was filled with the smell of overheated lubricating oil, I heard my mother say: 'And have you looked over here?' and over there was another big package with our names on it, and inside it was a 'Soccerado' set.

Sitting here in 2006, it actually brings a tear to my eye to imagine what it must have cost my parents in various sacrifices to give us both of these almost unthinkable treats. What I do feel sure of is that, if they'd known I'd be sitting here forty-six years later remembering it all so vividly, it would have confirmed for them that it had been worth it.

So what's all this got to do with being a Grumpy Old Man?

Good question, and let's pull ourselves together and find out. The thrill I'm describing was possible at that level of intensity only because we had nothing for the rest of the year. In this country, thank God, not many of today's kids go through the relative deprivation we had to go through in order for a treat at Christmas to be such an overwhelming thing. Those moments are gone, and they can't ever be like that again in our lives – not as kids and not as parents either, because our own children were always excited and grateful and delightful, but if I'm honest, at nothing like the same level.

Would I swap their lives as children for ours? Of course not – but none the less part of it makes you sad. Well, not sad exactly, but maybe just a little bit grumpy.

4

It's Not All Bad

Before we proceed any further, I thought we might pause for a moment to consider one or two of what Grumpy Old Men might regard as the particular merits of Christmas. Counter-intuitive, yes, controversial maybe, but let's go with the flow for a moment.

Many people make the mistake of thinking that Grumpy Old Men are grumpy. Miserable, complaining old sods who should properly be put out of their misery so that everyone else can get a break from the whingeing. But that's not true. Grumpy Old Men are not grumpy as it's formally defined. Not unhappy. Not even always moaning (though they do moan quite a lot).

No, what being a Grumpy Old Man really means, as many of us already know, is that we see the perverse and ridiculous in everyday situations which those non-afflicted seem to regard as normal. We question what everyone else seems to take for granted. We get amusement or irritation at stuff that passes everyone else by unnoticed.

So that when, for example, the commentator on Sky Sport says, 'Up next we've cricket', the rest of the world is hearing that the next thing on is cricket, and Rory McGrath is hearing about a game of cricket in which people weave, or something which is going up somewhere. And while the rest of you think nothing of it when you pass a sign on the road saying 'Hockstead, the brighter borough', Sir Tim Rice is asking, 'Brighter than what? Brighter than Merton? Brighter than it was yesterday?'

When everyone else around us hears a reference to 'complimentary tea and coffee' and thinks they are free, Grumpies are thinking of the tea and coffee that are included in the exorbitant price you've been charged but which at least say nice things about you. (Keep up keep up.) When we hear on the news (as I did this morning), 'The death sentence is mandatory but in this case the judge may commute it to life imprisonment', we want to go round to the back of the telly, unscrew the cover, reach in and strangle the newsreader.

See what I mean?

So, for example, one of the few things about this season which recommends it to me and some other Grumpy Old Men of my acquaintance is that it's the one time of year when we get to use and celebrate a whole vocabulary which modern life has made more or less redundant in our everyday lives. A whole load of words and phrases which, like the fairy with the sharp end of a Norwegian spruce stuck up her arse, pop out for the Christmas season and are then packed away for the whole of the remainder of the year. To recover.

Words that everyone else seems to just say and pass over without comment, but which are quite likely to make the Grumpy pause for thought. What sort of thing am I thinking of? Well, I'm thinking of words such as 'swaddling'.

Now just how wonderful a word is that? 'Swaddling.' Say it out loud with me: 'Swaddling.' With feeling now, and emphasising the individual syllables, 'SWO–DEL–LING.' I think you'll agree that it feels good to say, doesn't it? A happy collection of consonants that, when blended together and meandering around your teeth and tongue, sound as though they'll mean something cosy. 'They wrapped the baby in swaddling clothes' – which I seem to think means sort of 'tightly wrapped'.

I don't get to use the word 'swaddling' much in the eleven months of the year before December, and I think we should all try to do our level best to find a way to include it in our regular vocabulary. Not that I'm imagining the opportunities will be legion. The only time I use the term 'tightly wrapped' nowadays is when I'm making a derogatory comment about the brainpower of some broadcasting commissioning editor or other, as in 'I don't think he's all that tightly wrapped', and I don't think that 'swaddling' is going to be a useful substitute. But I'm going to make the effort, and so should you.

Another neglected and under-utilised word which is in fact rather adjacent to swaddling in this sense is, of course, 'manger'. 'Manger' isn't quite such a good word, is it? 'Manger.' It sounds a bit like something a sick dog might get. 'Manger' from the noun 'mange'. Or is it from the verb 'to mange'?

But how many kids, do you suppose, appear in nativity plays every year and talk about the baby Jesu being wrapped in swaddling clothes and laid in a manger, and have not the slightest idea what these words mean? Like swaddling, manger gets pulled out with the leftover crackers, used and abused with total abandon for a couple of weeks, and is then wrapped up and put back in its box until next year.

'Noel' is another good one. It seems that the first Noel that the angel did say was to certain poor shepherds in fields where they lay. It must have terrified the poor bastards. Can you imagine anything worse? You're sitting down at the end of a long day for a cuppa tea... Anyway, it's too soon to be diverted into all that. I think that 'Noel' is just another word for Christmas, isn't it? But 'Happy Noel' sounds so much better than 'Happy Christmas'. Or maybe that's just me.

A nice word that rarely gets trotted out other than at Christmas is 'tidings', which is another way of saying 'news'. This feels like another word we should get more use from. Can you imagine it? 'Shock tidings today from the Department of Education that pupils in England and Wales are going to be taught grammar and spelling.' Tidings of comfort and joy that would be indeed.

Yet another word that has had a few bad years is 'lo' as in 'lo, there appeared in the east a star' or whatever. What's all that about? When else do you hear sentences that include the word 'lo' – except maybe as in 'J-Lo', but that's another low. But 'lo' has a sense of style about it, doesn't it? Maybe newsreaders could start every story with 'lo'.

Jeremy Clarkson helpfully pointed out in our *Grumpy Old Men at Christmas* TV spectacular that these words are even harder to say in a Yorkshire accent. Try it at home. 'And lo, there appeared a star in the East and they did follow it.' In a Yorkshire accent. It's fun. Well, more fun anyway than most of the other stuff you're going to be doing around Christmas.

So now we're on a roll, I think. 'Gold' has always had a pretty good run for its money, but whatever happened to 'frankincense' and 'myrrh'? All of us must have wondered at one time or another what these items were, and generations of primary-school teachers have fobbed us off with 'some oriental perfume or spice' or something. But what were the three wise men doing bringing perfume and spices for a newborn infant anyway? You don't give the 'great smell of Brut', or turmeric to a new baby, do you? What could they have been thinking of? What about a nice rattle or a pink babygro with rabbits on the front? What about opening a savings account for the poor little mite?

In any event, frankincense and myrrh are weird ones, and I'm not holding out much hope that we're going to be able to squeeze them into much of the rest of the year. But it could be fun trying.

I mention all this partly because it helps us to understand the tortured mental processes of the Grumpy Old Man. Grumpiness, as we cannot be reminded too often, is not about being sad or miserable; it's about seeing the ridiculous in all the stuff that other people seem to accept without a remark or even a twitter. When everyone else is enjoying singing 'Gloria in excelsis deo', Grumpies are wondering what Gloria is doing in excelsis deo and just exactly where in the middle of the ludicrously extended first syllable of Gloria is a person supposed to pause for breath. And did anyone ever choke to death in the middle of singing it?

Better yet, when everyone else is enjoying singing about Good King Wenceslas, Grumpy Old Men are wondering who the hell was Good King Wenceslas, and how the fact that he just happened to glance out of the window at a particular moment came to justify the inclusion of this charming song in the great canon of English Christmas carols, all the rest of which seem to be more or less unambiguously about the birth of the baby Jesus. I'm betting that few of us can remember off by heart much past the first line of the second verse of 'Good King Wenceslas' – 'Bring me food and bring me wine,' etc., but up to that point there seems to be no specific mention of Jesus or anything. So what is all this doing up there alongside 'The First Noel' and 'Away in a Manger' at Christmas? (And if you know, please don't bother to write.)

So this is the burden we carry. Are we expecting any sympathy? No, not really, we just thought you should know that there are some things about Christmas that give Grumpy Old Men a little, and much-needed, lift. So anyway, let's press on with the stuff that doesn't.

5

Christmas Past
and Christmas Presents

Obviously in these latter years of my grumpiness, I've had very little to do with anything relating to the buying of presents at Christmas. We'll go into some of the reasons in a minute. However, before that it should be said in my defence that over earlier years I've done my share of participating in the decisions about what we might get for Lizzie's godmother, or Auntie Gladys, or the babysitter, or the brother-in-law or whomever.

When I say 'participated' I guess what I really mean is that I have played the part of the straight-man in what might easily pass for a scene from an early play by Samuel Beckett. It goes something like this:

SHE: Do you think Molly might like a scarf?
ME: Yes, I think she might.
SHE: I saw a nice one in Bentalls that she might like.
ME: Sounds like a good idea then.

SHE: Or do you think she might prefer a handbag?

ME: Yes, I'm sure she'd like a handbag.

SHE: It's just that her sister bought her a handbag last year, but it didn't go with that very nice coat she bought from the market.

ME: Maybe get her a new bag then?

SHE: We could do, but on the other hand she is still using the bag she brought back from Portugal, and the scarf I saw in Bentalls was very nice.

ME: Well, maybe the scarf then?

SHE: Perhaps I'll get the scarf, then if I change my mind, I can give it to Millie instead.

ME: Yes, good idea.

I could go on with this at some inordinate length – and then, who knows, I might end up with the Nobel prize for literature – but let's just assume that Godot has turned up and get to the bloody point. The point is that after several years of these discussions – about what to buy for Grandma, Hettie, the neighbours, etc. – my wife eventually worked out that they were a bit one-sided. After about ten years of it, in fact, she asked me one Christmas if I thought I'd ever contributed an original idea for what we might buy for someone.

I was mightily indignant at this outrage, and felt sure that I could think of loads of examples. Needless to say... Well, you know the rest.

The problems that Grumpy Old Men have with presents at Christmas start a long way back from all this. In fact they go right back to basics. Because it's one of the many terrible afflictions faced up to on a daily, nay hourly, basis by Grumpy Old Men, that we just can't stop ourselves from asking questions.

Obviously by that I don't mean stupid questions like: 'Can you tell me the way to King's Cross?' or 'Have you got this in beige?' No no, I mean that one aspect of the persecution that is the life of a Grumpy is that we are continuously asking questions about stuff that everyone else in the world seems to regard as straightforward and obvious, but which strikes us as ridiculous.

For example, do you ever use the AA route-finder? You'll type in the postcodes of your departure point and your destination, and hey presto you get a rather over-detailed but none the less useful set of directions. Cool, and that would be fine, except that someone has decided to take this opportunity to tell you that driving long distances without a break can be dangerous, and that you should ensure that you take proper rests.

Whereas this passes most people by, the Grumpy Old Man is yelling 'Fuck right off!' or perhaps something slightly more erudite.

'Do you think we need you to tell us that we should take a rest from driving now and then? And did anyone ever, in the whole of human history, intend to drive through the night, but change their minds when they read this little warning?' Of course they bloody well didn't.

Or when I see the little caption in the corner of the TV screen in an advertisement for some alcoholic drink that says 'Enjoy sensibly', I want to ask what the hell has it got to do with them if I use it sensibly or not? On the fairly rare occasions that I want to drink a lot of alcohol, it's because at that moment I don't want to be sensible at all. Probably at that moment I want to be very silly, so you can take your 'enjoy sensibly' advice and insert it.

In these little examples we've gone directly to the heart of it. If you're reading this and thinking 'What on earth is this twat on about?', then you are very probably not a true Grumpy and maybe, you can hope, you never will be. If you can't see anything in this, you may be affliction-free, in which case thank your lucky stars. Because Grumpies will recognise this phenomenon at 100 yards. Maybe not necessarily in these instances but in the sort of thing.

To everyone else it seems either obvious or unremarkable; to a Grumpy it's a source of bewilderment at best and downright irritation at worst. Everyone else just hears it and passes on; Grumpies can't stop themselves from asking idiot questions.

OK, so you may be wondering what is the relevance of all this preliminary guff to the subject of Christmas presents, and here comes the point. Whereas everyone else takes it for granted, we have a question. Why is it, do you think, that we give presents to each other at Christmas?

No, seriously, I know it's an odd thing to ask, because we all think of Christmas and present-giving as more or less synonymous; but why do you think that is? Giving presents to other people is, if you think about it, rather an odd thing to do anyway. Let's analyse it for a moment.

You've gone out and worked very hard for a long time to earn this money, have already given away a bit less than half of it to the government, and have put whatever's left into your bank account; Then, instead of using it to pay the rent, or buy food, or get the car serviced or go on holiday, you've decided to go out and buy an item which is probably total bloody rubbish to give to someone else on Christmas morning. They are going to take it from you, unwrap it, say 'thank you', and then they're going to put it in their cupboard until next year when they are probably going to give it away to someone else. Unless of course, you also give them the receipt, in which case you could have cut out all the effort in the middle and just handed over the money you earned in the first place.

A bit cynical? Maybe, but you've got to admit that when I put it like that, it does seem a very weird thing to do. Don't you think?

To be honest, I reckon that buying presents for other people is a weird thing to do even on their birthday. However, I suppose that on your birthday you have in some strange sense achieved something. Your birthday is something that is specifically about you that could, I suppose, be marked by giving you a present.

So why would you give people presents at Christmas? If it's anyone's birthday at all, it's Jesus's, not yours. If anyone is going to get a present, it should be him, not you. So maybe this would be a good time to dig deep into the pockets and give money to the church or a charity. (Without telling anyone please.)

But what did you do to deserve a present at Christmas? Eh?

Anyway, for some reason I can't immediately think of or work out, it's been decided that at Christmas we all give each other presents. And this I think is a contender for the worst thing about Christmas for a Grumpy.

It's not that a Grumpy doesn't like giving presents. Despite the reputation of being miserly old misery-guts that some of us endure, a Grumpy Old Man is as pleased as anyone to see genuine delight on the face of anyone he doesn't actively dislike. It's not even that a Grumpy doesn't like receiving presents, although it has to be said that the ratio of presents received to those genuinely appreciated is usually fairly unfavourable.

No, it's not about the giving and the receiving, it is of course about the *shopping*. Giving and receiving – well, we can't work out why we do it, but if we're going to do it, that's fine. We'll go with it. It's the *shopping for the presents* that's the problem.

Here comes a simple truth that every Grumpy Old Man, and every partner of a Grumpy Old Man, knows as clearly as they know their own names. We hate shopping. We just hate it, and over the years we've made ourselves so unpleasant and obnoxious when coerced into going, that by and large our loved ones would rather do anything than go shopping with us.

And bear in mind that the sole redeeming feature about regular week-to-week shopping is that in an ordinary circumstance a Grumpy Old Man will know exactly what it is that he wants to buy. In an ordinary circumstance, shopping for a Grumpy Old Man involves knowing what he wants, going to the shop, buying it and coming home again. Now doesn't it?

Take the example of a Grumpy Old Man

wanting to buy a pullover. What do you call it in your house? Jumper? Sweater? Anyway, one of those woolly things with arms and a hole for your neck. If a bloke wants to buy a pullover, he's going to go directly to his favourite shop, which is likely to be the one where he can park most easily and which ponces about the least. He's going to find something in the colour he wants, that looks warm enough, and that fits. He's going to pay for it and go home. Job done, now what's on the telly?

How does that compare with his partner when undertaking a similar objective?

Well, leaving aside for the moment that a shopping trip for a woman is not so much a shopping trip but a day out in which she can look around for the stuff she wants, meet a friend for coffee, saunter about for a couple of hours, then go and sit in Café Revive or whatever it is and eat an egg and cress sandwich; leaving all that aside, the shopping trip is not necessarily regarded as a failure if nothing is bought. In fact, it might be more accurate to describe a lot of these outings as 'fact finding'.

First of all, every shop that sells pullovers within a three-mile radius has to be prospected. This one has a sale on but their stuff isn't usually as good, this one doesn't have a sale and is much more expensive but by and large it's better quality. This one had a very nice one in a charcoal colour but it had a little fleck in it which she's not sure about. On the other hand, it did also have some quite nice ribbing around the collar which they didn't have in that one that caught the eye in the first shop. This one was nice but when tried on turned out to be a bit loose on the shoulders.

Eventually a pullover may be selected and paid for, but that by no means means that the purchase is confirmed. (We're just exploring how many meanings 'means' can have, by the way.) It may come home, and it may stay in the bag in the hallway for up to a fortnight, but then is very likely to go back in favour of one that her friend Laura told her about that she'd seen in that little shop that's just opened in Wimbledon.

When I get the monthly invoice for our stuff at John Lewis or wherever, I'll scan the three pages or so of items in absolute horror, concluding that the final total must be in the thousands. Then when I get there I'm often pleasantly surprised to find that it can be about a third of what I expect it to be – just because there are nearly as many refunds as there are purchases. At least a third of the stuff that comes home eventually goes back to the store, and once or twice there has been more going back than coming home – which has left me in credit.

Anyway, that's how a woman shops, and

it's nothing like how a man shops. But it is, however, exactly the kind of shopping a bloke has to do if he is trying to buy Christmas presents for someone else and doesn't have a clue what to get. A lot of 'browsing'. Grumpy Old Men don't want to 'browse'; we want to get what we want and get home.

So apart from not having a clue what to buy, and hating the idea of 'browsing', what in particular is it about Christmas shopping that Grumpy Old Men don't like? Well, let's see if we can think of anything ... For Grumpies of a sensitive disposition, we recommend a bit of deep breathing to get through what follows.

There's being reminded that we promised to go, running out of excuses on a Saturday morning and finally having to go, sitting in a long queue of traffic on the way to the shops which is remarkably similar to the queue of traffic you sit in every other day of the week on your way to work. Then there's queuing for about forty-five minutes to get into the multi-storey car park, and getting into an argument with the bloke in the Fiat who has dived into the space you had just gone past but were clearly indicating your intention to reverse into. (Deep breath recommended here.)

There's trying to manoeuvre your way around about a quarter of a million women who are out with their mothers. Then there's

67

traipsing around looking in endless shop windows, all of which look remarkably similar to each other, and all of which have far too much choice of whatever it is you might want to buy so that you are totally confused. There's having no idea what to get, trying to attract the attention of the poor harassed sod who's supposed to be serving, getting no useful help, and eventually buying something more out of exhaustion and desperation than desire. (Another big breath required here, I'm afraid.)

There's the returning to the car park and standing in a queue behind seventeen people at the pay-station. After about half of your lifespan has passed, you watch the woman in front of you trying to put her ticket into the machine, except that she's holding it upside down so that it keeps going in and coming out again. You are wondering whether to point this out to her, but she's from Poland and you fear that any intervention on your part may be misunderstood and indeed may make matters worse. When eventually she gets it right, the machine swallows the ticket and she stands looking at it and waiting for something else to happen. You are about to point out the little window that says '£7.50' when she spots it herself and then, and only then, starts looking for her purse. She takes out a series of small denomination coins one at a time, and by the time she's managed to do so the clock has ticked past another hour which has added a further £2 to the already exorbitant price of your short stay in the car park. (Still breathing?)

You, of course, have your ticket ready. You put it in the machine the right way up, and have the correct coins available to insert. However, you are then treated to the unmistakable sound of your coins tumbling through the machine and landing in the 'reject coins' tray. You are unable to fathom why this should be, but after about three tries, eventually the machine accepts the ransom and your ticket is returned to you safe and unharmed.

You go back to the car, queue at the barrier to get out, only to find that – despite about a million signs making it clear – the bloke in front of you apparently didn't realise that he can't pay on exit, and so you have to reverse to let him back. You can't work out what is the appropriate hand gesture to the bloke behind you to indicate that you want to reverse because the bloke in front of you is an idiot. (Keep breathing; we're on the home straight now.)

Eventually he gets it, and you then watch him trying to work out a similar gesture for the bloke behind him. At last you emerge into daylight and sit in another traffic queue on your way back, finally arriving home three hours later, exhausted, pissed off and without any sense of having achieved anything whatsoever.

Any of that ring a bell?

So that's the mechanics of it. Now let's move on to the problems that Grumpies have in knowing what to buy.

Having over the years made some of my most catastrophic mistakes in this area, I've spent quite a long time wondering why it is that men are so useless at Christmas shopping. And in my case I've worked out that I just don't have the facility to put myself in the place of someone else – even someone I'm fairly close to and know well – and work out what it is they're going to want.

How do people do it? Do you try to put yourself into their minds? Try to see the world from their point of view and say, 'If I were them, what would I want?' I sincerely don't know how to do that. I have no way of knowing if this is easy or hard for most ordinary people, but for me and Grumpies like me it's damned nearly impossible.

Take something like a piece of jewellery. It's well known that women don't wear jewellery to please or catch the eye of men; they wear jewellery to impress other women or to make them jealous. An unattractive truth, I'm afraid, but I don't think you'll find any honest person to seriously challenge it. By and large men have no idea about jewellery. In my case, if you showed me a piece of jewellery now and then showed me the same piece in about an hour and asked me if it was the same item, I'd have no idea. It doesn't register in our consciousness. We don't get it, and we don't care.

Therefore, even if we've lived with the same person for a couple of decades or more, we've probably got very little idea about what sort of jewellery she wears or would like. That's why, on the odd occasion that men are stupid enough to buy jewellery for their partners, they usually buy it by the gram. They think the bigger the stone, the more impressed everyone will be, and the more generous they will seem.

I suspect that there may be an element of truth in that as far as diamonds are concerned, but I don't sense that it has much validity for anything else. Anyhow, that's by the by. The point is that in jewellery, as in so many other things, a man will very rarely have any idea of what his wife or partner will really like.

So my catastrophic lack of any facility for getting the right thing, or indeed anything close to the right thing, has led over the years to some real horror stories. Like all men, I would always leave it to the last minute, and then I'd scurry out on Christmas Eve, frantically searching for something, anything, to buy that she might conceivably like.

I tried, heaven knows I tried, clumping around amidst the leather goods or the knitwear, slouching among the biographies and the address books. But I swear I really don't think that in all the years I was trying to do it, I ever got anything right. Not ever. Not anything.

To be fair to myself, I don't think I've ever been stupid enough to believe you can say 'I love you' with a bread-maker, or that anything with the word 'Dyson' written on it can be an acceptable Christmas gift. What do you take me for? However, over the years I've managed to buy inappropriate purses, handbags, necklaces, make-up, perfume, potpourri, books, videos, picture-frames, stationery and CDs – to name but a few.

My wife used to be pretty good at dealing with this. On Christmas morning she'd carefully open any presents from me, would 'ooh' and 'aah' at all the appropriate junctures, would express enormous surprise and pleasure, and say that whatever ridiculous item I'd bought was exactly what she wanted. All with a sincerity that I truly believe would have fooled the FBI. Then she would pack these items tidily away, so that it was only maybe six months later that I'd remember, or find whatever it was hidden away in a drawer.

'I see you haven't used that handbag I bought you.'

'No, to tell you the truth, it doesn't really go with anything I've got,' which I realised only then was her polite way of telling me that she wouldn't be seen dead carrying something that looked like a highly polished tortoise, or whatever. 'You didn't by any chance keep the receipt, did you?'

Anyway, after about fifteen years of this fiasco – by which time I had wholeheartedly adopted the Grumpy Old Man frame of mind – I proposed a new arrangement. At any time throughout the year that my wife would see something she thought she might like to have as a present, she would buy it, and stash it away to receive from me for Christmas. So that these days, on Christmas Eve, she hands me several carrier bags – full of things I never would have bought for her in a million years – and I conscientiously wrap them up and put them under the tree for the following morning.

We still go through a strange ritualistic charade in which she pretends that she doesn't know what something is, but at least this time there is a fair chance that when she says, 'That's just what I wanted', it is just what she wanted.

And by this circuitous route eventually we arrived at our current much more satisfactory arrangement for all concerned, which is that I play no part whatsoever in the question of what we buy for anyone. In that way my wife can do what she really likes to do best – which is to start her Christmas shopping round about January.

Yes, that's right; just as I have a constant stream of invective going around my brain, bubbling away beneath the surface of whatever it is I'm apparently doing, my wife has this facility for meandering around shops throughout the year and occasionally spotting something and thinking, 'that would do for Auntie Gloria at Christmas.' Extraordinary, isn't it? And damnably clever too. Because what it means is that by the time we get to November, if the subject comes up at all, she is able to declare that she has already managed to buy most of our Christmas presents.

She bought a handbag for her mother in the January sales, a scarf for Miren when we had that weekend away in Spain, and a nice jumper for Helen when we went to that factory outlet in Wilton last June. That wallet I saw in a shop in March and casually made a rare favourable comment about but which entirely went out of my mind is among my little collection of parcels.

I know that this sort of thing can easily cause resentment in the households of Grumpies. I recall that very funny writer – Jane Moore, is it? – saying in an episode of *Grumpy Old Women* that her husband would sometimes ask her, 'What have we bought for Margery?' and she'd reply, 'I don't know what *you've* bought for Margery, but *I've* bought her a...' whatever it was. This doesn't happen in our household because by and large my wife has worked out that life is much simpler leaving me out of these things altogether. We have a clear division of labour; a fair allocation of tasks which has been finely honed over the years to recognise our various aptitudes and abilities.

For example, I renew the household and the fire insurance, and she buys and cooks all the food. I make sure that the cars are serviced, get new tyres, are MOTd etc. and she ensures that the kids go to school and are fed and clothed. I decide whether we're going to recognise the new government in Azerbaijan and she buys the presents at Christmas. I think any fair-minded person would agree that this is a reasonable division of effort.

So at this point, just before we stop thinking about presents for a little while, I was planning to invent a long and no doubt highly entertaining narrative about the mad panic and scramble there always is to get hold of whatever is the Christmas toy for the kids that has been hyped beyond all sense and reason, and is in short supply.

You know the sort of stuff, Cabbage-patch dolls or My Little Pony dressing table or Segga-megga-x-box-plus or whatever the hell it is. A load of stuff has been written and said about this – in fact I believe that recently an entire feature film was made about it. However, as this is intended to be read only between friends, why not tell the truth? And the truth is that, even before I really entered my grumpy years – thirty-five or so onwards – I was far too grumpy ever to participate in all that shit.

That's right. Even in my years as a young Dad who was probably as devoted to the kids as most people, I always drew the line at joining in that unseemly and preposterous saga of learning that Toys-Я-Us had run out of PlayStations but that they were expecting a small number in on Wednesday, and going down and laying siege to the place among hordes of other lame-brains. No, I believe that by and large we did the best we could, and I think it's fair to say that the kids haven't grown up to be unusually maladjusted as a result of any particular deprivation of that sort.

That's not to say that they're not maladjusted, and no doubt in years to come both Matt and Lizzie will be found lying on the psychiatrist's couch complaining that they are unable to sustain a committed relationship because they missed out one year on the Barbie Castle or whatever the hell it was, but hey, what are you going to do?

No, you're relieved of the task of reading a

load of invective about the annual horror at Hamleys, or terror at Toys-Я-Us. Let's take a pass, and get onto something else.

6

Parties

The best thing about the whole Grumpy Old Man experience for me over the last few years has been the realisation that it's not just me after all.

Time was when I, like just about every other Grumpy Old Man I've spoken to, thought that maybe I was the only one going around with that continual running commentary in my head. You know the sort of thing: 'Look at that wanker dressed in all that lycra; must be Lance Armstrong on his way to work'; or 'Who decided that I needed to see a road-sign with an illuminated smiley face if I'm driving at 28 mph past the school or a grimacing one if I'm doing 32?'; or 'When will someone invent a sticker for the car window that says "What does it matter who's on board"?'

Anyway, you get the idea. That's the sort of stuff that I can't get out of my head as I'm going about my daily business, and it's been a huge relief for me to learn that exactly the same stuff goes through the heads of Grumpy Old Men as diverse as Arthur Smith and Sir Tim Rice, Bob Geldof and Sir Gerry Robinson, Lemm Sissay and Bill Nighy. We all think more or less the same stuff, more or less all the time. About the bollocks that surrounds us.

And it's not just the 'celebrities' who have appeared in the programmes either. When I first day-dreamed up the Grumpy Old Man notion, I tried it out on all my mates of a certain age and a certain disposition, and was amazed to learn that people I thought I knew reasonably well were all the time secretly suffering under a strikingly similar set of persecutions as I do. Being irritated to the point of distraction by otherwise sensible musicians who talk shite when they should be playing music, for example. Or idiotic footballers who talk shite when they should be playing football. Or magazines which insist on writing shite about the full-of-shite lives of airhead 'celebrities'. Or politicians who just talk shite all the time.

A huge relief. We all think the same thing. Except...

Except that I still fear that it may be just me who feels as grumpy as I do about parties. Birthday parties, anniversary parties, wedding parties and, of course, Christmas parties.

Even after all the camaraderie of grumpiness, the shared horror of instruction manuals, call-centres, self-assembly furniture etc., it does still seem to me that, with a few honourable exceptions among the very hardcore Grumpy Old Men of my acquaintance, most of the otherwise apparently sane GOMs I know seem to enjoy a party.

If they didn't, why would they keep giving them? Why would they keep attending them?

I've talked before about the long list of excuses my wife has invented over the years for why I'm unable to attend Lizzie's fortieth, or Lawrence's fiftieth, or Nick and Annabelle's engagement or Frank's retirement party. I've often encouraged her to simply tell people that 'He's a grumpy old bastard and couldn't be arsed to come', and I know that she has resorted to that with her best and closest friends. But usually she'll come up with something plausible that saves her the embarrassment of everyone knowing that she's got a cantankerous old sod for a husband.

However, at Christmastime, that's not so straightforward. While I might easily have a 'long-term-commitment-he-could-not-get-out-of' to an industry event when Iris is having her soirée on the 17th, wouldn't it be too much of a coincidence if I also had to visit an aged aunt who's been unexpectedly taken ill in Leatherhead when Laura is having people

79

round on the 18th? And then an unbreakable appointment to change my library books when Liz and Brian are 'at home' on the 19th?

You see the problem? Finding excuses to miss the odd summer barbecue dotted around various weekends through June, July and August is one thing, but it's the concentration of these execrable events in the few weeks coming up to Christmas that gives rise to a range of ever-more-extravagant alibis.

But why is it only me that feels the need to go to such lengths to avoid these occasions? What about all those other blokes? Every bit as grumpy as I am in every other respect, can they possibly enjoy these events? Can they want to go? How could they?

Think about it for a minute. It's two weeks before Christmas. In most businesses it's a busy time of year because you've got a whole load of stuff to get finished before the holiday break which used to last two days, then spread out into the week between Christmas and New Year's Day, and now seems to stretch from the weekend before Christmas Eve to the weekend after New Year's Day. So you're frantically busy, and that would be bad enough, but all the while you're trying to deal with 'frantic', various other parts of your industry which take life less seriously than you do but with whom you have to deal are breaking out into festive spirit.

You'll call to find out when to expect an urgent delivery and hear the sounds of revelling in the background as some drunken idiot writes down the message you are dictating on the back of someone's knickers – or something.

So at the end of an especially 'frantic' midweek day, what do you want to do when you get home? Well, you may be able to guess what I want to do. I want to take off my shoes, have my dinner, grab a glass of wine and a bowl of olives and sit in front of a DVD of *Curb Your Enthusiasm*. Then I want to go to bed whenever I feel like it. That's my idea of an agreeable evening.

What I assuredly do not want to do when I get home after said very hard day of work dealing with 'frantic' is to be told that I'm not going to be getting any dinner because Lena has spent the last week preparing hors d'oeuvres, and that I have just about got time to have a shower and get changed before we have to head out again into the traffic I've just driven through.

I'm not going into the whole saga that takes place next; suffice to say it mostly focuses on whether I have to shave (I do), whether I can wear my jeans (I can't), whether I need to change this shirt (I do), and whether that jackass from the sports-supply business that I got stuck with last year will be there again (he will), etc., etc.

And the thing that creases me is that, when we get there, we find that we know everyone. Just about all of them were at the party we went to on Thursday, so we know all their news, and they know us and all of ours, and therefore we're going to spend about three hours with a single glass of wine in hand (because I'm driving and anyway have got to deal with 'frantic' again tomorrow morning) trying to think of something else to say.

How much fun is that?

It has to be said that women are much better at this than men. Within about five seconds of arriving, half a dozen of them are in a group talking about a very nice pair of stud earrings that Margery bought in that little jewellers just off Market Square; you know the one, with all the diamond rings in the window, the bloke who runs it is a bit effeminate-looking. It doesn't seem to matter that they met yesterday, and the day before, and maybe even at lunchtime today; they've still got loads of stuff to talk about. 'What are you getting for Eric for Christmas? Yes I know, mine's difficult to buy for as well.' They have a shared sense of comradeship born of the fact that they've got us to deal with – and so they talk about us as if we're pet gorillas.

'Mine says he wants a drum kit but I said to him, where on earth are we going to put a drum kit; and anyway, he's just reliving his lost youth.'

'Better relive it with a drum kit than the other way... Mine says he's thinking he wants to buy a sports car.' They all look at each other with that 'we-all-know-what-that-means' look.

Men can't do any of this. We can't even have the conversation about 'Which way did you come?' because we all live about three miles apart and there's only one route in or out. We can talk about the traffic, and how it's only getting worse, and we do – at length. Then each of us contributes an anecdote about how his own journey to work has deteriorated in the last few months. Then we all agree that it's a conspiracy.

There's also a bit to say about the football, or the cricket or the rugby, but I don't really give much of a toss about any of those, so I don't have a lot to offer. And then if we're not careful, we're talking about 'How's business?' and you're trying to show an interest in something you're not remotely interested in, and you don't want to talk about your own stuff because if you do you might as well be back at work.

Unlike our partners, we're no good at talking to each other about our ailments, or about a shirt we might recently have purchased, or even much about how the kids are doing at school. We don't compare notes about the doctor, or the butcher or that new teacher at the school with the nose-stud who thinks she's super-cool but the kids love her. We just don't.

I'm not going to go into details of what these parties are like; partly because you know, and partly because I described one such occasion in great detail on 22 December of *The Secret Diary*. (It feels a bit self-regarding to reference something else I've written myself, but I reckon that on balance it's better to be accused of that than to be accused of subjecting you to a very similar load of old bile twice.)

Anyway the new thing is that in this year just gone, for some reason only she could guess at, my wife decided that we needed to hold one of these events at our house. God knows why – maybe because we've lived in this neighbourhood for about ten years and have never done so yet. Usually, sometime around October, my wife mentions that she thinks we should hold a party this coming Christmas, but over the following weeks my general lack of enthusiasm for the idea wears her down, and no more is said about it. However, this time she seemed determined.

Around the middle of November she told me the proposed date, and read me a list of her friends and their husbands to whom she was going to send invitations (like I'm interested). At the same time she asked me which of 'my friends' I wanted to invite and, do you know, I couldn't think of anyone.

Funnily enough, it's not that I don't have any friends. Despite what must seem to the dispassionate reader to be my totally unendearing and antisocial nature, I am not a total 'billy-no-mates'. However, the truth is that I see a lot of my friends via work, and so the very last thing we all want to do in our spare time is get together again. Several of my other mates live in Manchester, or Salisbury or Newcastle, and I doubt if they would be consumed with enthusiasm at the prospect of travelling hundreds of miles for this no-doubt momentous occasion. Several others live right over in north-east London and would welcome the idea of schlepping over to our place on a weekday evening about us much as I'd welcome going over to theirs.

So, to come to the point, this last Christmas we had a little evening *chez nous*, to which all my wife's friends were invited; and funnily enough, all but a couple of them came. I was impressed by that, considering that it's a busy time of year and all, but my wife explained that mostly they will have been driven by curiosity. How does someone famous for being a totally grumpy bastard host a party?

I probably shouldn't go into great detail, because, though I don't give a bugger, my wife does, and it's a bit rude even by my standards to invite a whole load of people to your house and then describe all their foibles in print. On the other hand, what's the worst thing that can happen? I won't be invited to their place next year? Let's take the risk...

First of all there's Jeremy. Jeremy is married to Babs and is a designer. When I first heard that Jeremy was a designer I thought something like, 'Well that'll be interesting.' I was thinking cars, aeroplanes, hovercrafts. Or if not anything quite so 'boy's toys', then maybe something interesting like aircraft seats, or possibly even the sets for TV shows. 'Designer,' I thought, 'maybe he and I might be able to find something to talk about.'

Well, take a minute and see if you can guess what Jeremy designs. I know that sounds an outlandish suggestion. It could be anything, but funnily enough, I think if you try hard enough you'll probably get it. What could Jeremy design that would have enough aspects to it to enable him to go on and on and on about it for the best part of two and a half hours, but which in itself is about as interesting as a not very interesting thing being described to you by a very boring person?

The answer is cup-holders. Did you get it? Cup-holders. In this particular case, a cup-holder which you can buy at a DIY store to attach to any surface that requires a cup-holder, but which folds down flat when you aren't using it. Three pieces of plastic fastened together and a small spring.

Jeremy is a pointed little bloke with hairs growing vivaciously out of his ears and nostrils who talks energetically and effusively and effervescently and endlessly about the design of cup-holders. Take it from me, if there is a Nobel prize for endless wittering, Jeremy is your man. And he was at our party.

Or then there is Frank. Frank is married to Beth – or at least we think they're married, but something Beth said to my wife recently suggested that maybe they aren't. Or anyway that Frank and Beth may not be an item for much longer, which is a shame because Frank and Beth have two teenage kids and three dogs. Dividing up two kids is easy enough, but how do you divide up three dogs? (Into six equal parts would be my answer, but probably we shouldn't go there.)

Anyway Frank is something in local government. I know that because I've heard Frank talk about it on several occasions, for about an hour and a half each time, and I still am not clear what he actually does. Mostly what he does is to exercise total contempt for the elected councillors who run the place, and if even a quarter of his stories are true, the rest of us should have contempt too.

Frank and Beth came to the party we had at our house just before Christmas and Frank talked about the Local Structure Plan for an amount of time approximately equal to the time it takes to do the marathon in a deep-sea-diver's outfit.

However, despite all that, in spite of Jeremy and in spite of Frank, I have to report that, for the Grumpy Old Man, giving a party may turn out to be less vexatious than attending one. The reason I say that is that you don't get stuck with people. You can wander around, with a bottle of white wine in one hand and a bottle of red wine in the other hand, filling up glasses, pretending to be affable and then moving swiftly on. And if someone does metaphorically grab hold of you and start regaling you with an hilarious anecdote about the sales conference in Filey, you can conveniently spot someone else on the other side of the room who desperately needs a drink, and promise to come by and hear the rest of the anecdote later. Then the only problem is how to avoid that particular person for the whole of the rest of the evening, while making sure that their drink is topped up.

Of course, the obvious downside of hosting your own party is that you don't get the option of leaving early and heading off home to bed. Chances are that the first people will start to leave at a reasonable hour because they've got to get up early the next morning – or more probably are as bored with you as you are with them. Then a few others will drift away and you start to feel reasonably hopeful of getting to bed before the sun comes up. But almost inevitably at least one couple will show no signs whatever of leaving, and indeed when you run out of things to say and your wife stupidly mentions the possibility of a nightcap, will say 'What a nice idea'.

The worst thing of all is when this couple, who have been wandering around and mingling with your other guests for the first three hours of the evening, decide that this is the moment to sit down on the settee. They want to start talking about your other guests and how 'Roxanne looked a bit peaky' or how 'I thought maybe she and Pete had had a row before they came'.

This is too much for me. When a version of this happened at our party, I cleared away the worst of the debris and then popped my head in the living room and said, 'Goodnight.' My wife looked at me as though I'd stabbed her in the back, which in a way I suppose I had – but hey, they were her friends.

A whole different set of vexations and humiliations applied to the party we held at the office. So much has been written about the horrors of office parties that I suspect that there is little fresh to say about the perspective of the Grumpy Old Man. However, a little inhibition like that wouldn't usually stop us.

But before I start, I have a question. Yes, it's one of those Grumpy Old Men questions that doesn't occur to any normal person, but is the sort of thing that inevitably arises in the mind of a GOM. Is it just one of those apocryphal anecdotes that may have happened once at some place and some time in the past and has spread around the world like bird flu, or has anyone ever actually been to a party where the girls sit on photocopiers and take photocopies of their bums?

I only ask because I seem to have heard versions of this story year after year for a hundred years, and I believe I even saw an item in what passes for a local TV news programme about drunken women hoisting themselves onto the photocopier and pressing the green button. I think the news item was about a warning from photocopier manufacturers about the (I would have thought obvious) dangers of shards of glass in the arse area. However, I've never knowingly been at a party where this kind of thing has taken place, or spoken to anyone who has. Thank God.

No, the only office parties I've been to are the ones where the office creep, who's spent 364 days of the past year greasing and grovelling for a promotion, takes this opportunity to get massively drunk, lean on your shoulder, breathe beery breath into your face and tell you that the company you're really rather proud of is actually a bucket of shite. Or where, if you are the boss, you are aware of a gaggle of office juniors daring the bold one, who is showing an unwise amount of cleavage, to come up and ask you to dance. And although you want to dance with the bold office junior about as intensely as you want to undergo elective surgery to your scrotum using rusty instruments, you have to seem all good-humoured and go along with it. Or where Malcolm from Accounts, who has remained tightly within his shell for the past year, chooses this moment to do the routine that no one could possibly imagine that he's been perfecting, of the strippers' scene from *The Full Monty*.

So no, my belief is that the genuine Grumpy Old Man, the Republican Guard of the type, does not want to give parties and does not want to attend parties. Mostly what he wants at Christmas, rather like the rest of the time actually, is to be left a-bloody-lone.

However, if you are thinking of giving a party this Christmas, and you recognise some Grumpy Old Man among your guest list, perhaps we could perform a service to the nation by offering some tips which would be likely to make him slightly more agreeable as a guest. They're only suggestions, mind, to be used at your discretion; but we're here to help.

1 Write on the invitation card the time you actually want your guests to arrive. Funnily enough, quite a few of the Grumpy Old Men I know are punctual. I am, and therefore we tend to arrive at events sometime close to the time that we've been asked to arrive, and therefore it's not unknown for us to have to sit in the car, or drive round the streets, to wait for an acceptable degree of lateness. How stupid is that?

2 Newsflash: it's not possible to hold a glass, a plate, a napkin and a vol-au-vent in your hands at the same time. Something's got to give, and those silly little plastic things that you're supposed to clip over the edge of your plate invite disaster.

3 Most GOMs like hot and greasy little sausages on sticks, and even those rather poncy little fish and chip concoctions if they're served hot, but we hate those little pastry things with what tastes like warm mushroom soup in the middle. Apart from the fact that the paste burns the roof of the mouth, flaky stuff also sticks to your lips, your clothes and goes all over the carpet. And anyway, they taste like something you scraped off the walls of the oven.

4 No one wants to hear any speeches, even short ones, on any subject; but if you're going to insist on it, remember that people can't easily applaud and hold a wine-glass at the same time.

5 If your grumpy guest is standing on his own looking miserable, that's his usual look and doesn't necessarily mean he's miserable; but if he is, introducing him to an idiot is unlikely to cheer him up.

6 If he's talking to someone, it may be because he has already identified the only person in the room whose conversation he would prefer to a root-canal treatment. Leave him alone.

7 Tell him and his wife that it's perfectly OK to leave early.

There, I think that if you follow these seven simple rules, it'll help to make next year's Christmas parties go with more of a swing. Don't you?

7

The Tree

We've been talking from time to time in this book about some of the weird things that happen at Christmas which never happen at any other time. You know, like 'goodwill to all men' or drunks singing outside your house and expecting to be paid instead of reported to the police. The strange bits of irrationality which overcome people who are usually perfectly normal and relatively sensible for the rest of the year.

For example, what is it about Christmas that makes us want to destroy a perfectly good tree and bring it into the house?

I blame Prince Albert for this. Usually, by and large, I regard the royal family as a more or less interesting diversion, there to provide fairly harmless entertainment for the rest of us, but with no actual point. Sure, Prince Charles is a bit of a prat, but if you tried to think of any tangible effect he's had on your life, you'd be struggling, now wouldn't you?

And though I'm not particularly a student of the British monarchy, I've watched some of those endless ravings by that pompous Oxford history professor with the plummy voice, and as I ponder it now, I can't really think of much that any of them did that impinges directly on my day-to-day. I don't mean stuff like their heads on your coins or anything; I mean a real effect.

However, that doesn't apply to Prince Albert and Christmas trees. No, I think it's fairly clear that he introduced the notion of Christmas trees into Britain – in around 1846 in fact – and before then we'd been able to find a way to celebrate Christmas without schlepping into the forest with an axe, cutting down a perfectly good and healthy tree, dragging it back, sticking it in a pot, putting loads of shiny rubbish on it and then looking at it. Yes, we'd managed it somehow.

When you think about it like that, it does seem a very odd thing to do, now doesn't it? It's another one of those things we do every year, most of us without thinking too much about it, but if and when we do think about it, we can't for the life of us imagine why we would. What has a Christmas tree got to do with Christmas? Jesus will never even have seen a spruce, let alone advocated uprooting millions of them every year so that they could shed their needles in your car and you could go on finding them in the turn-ups of your trousers for months to come.

What's it all about? When you ask the question, people tend to just look skywards and say 'It's tradition'. Well, is it bollocks tradition – 1846? I don't call that tradition. I call that recent. From the perspective of my rapidly advancing years, it comes under the heading of 'very recent'. And anyway, what sort of an explanation is 'tradition' anyway?

It's ridiculous enough that we should do it at all, but our question for today is: why should it be, do we think, that men in general and, it seems, Grumpy Old Men in particular, always buy a tree that's far too big for the house? Why do we think that should be?

Is it that when we're out, we for some

reason want the chancer on the side of the road who's set up this little black-economy business for a couple of weeks to think that we live in a stately home? I doubt it – if we did manage to convince him of that he'd probably come round to rob us.

Is it that the smell of the pine needles temporarily robs us of our sense of space – so that one whiff of it and we imagine our ceilings to be two feet higher than they are? I doubt it.

No, I think the answer is that there's something about all this shit that brings out the latent lumberjack in us. Somewhere in the depths of our subconscious, we're some sort of frontiersmen. We'd like to think of ourselves as having put on those checked shirts and strange woolly peaked caps, slung a huge axe over our shoulder, and walked out into the forest to fell a mighty spruce – and then dragged it back home to suburbia to stick it in the corner of the living room.

The only trouble is that when you get it home and want to put it up in your living room or wherever, you have to cut six inches off the bottom, another six inches off the top, and then everyone in the household has to do a detour round it for the whole two weeks, before you have to take it down again.

These days I'm very grumpy about Christmas trees, and don't want one. We still have to have one, of course, but at least it can be the subject of a brief debate. However, when the kids were small it wasn't a matter for debate, and so we did what every other family in Britain does – I was going to say 'religiously', but I think we've already established that there's nothing religious about it.

For what seems like weeks before Christmas, you're driving past greengrocers and market stalls and pub car parks and garden nurseries and disused shops and little unused corners of the road, and seeing a bloke with a blackboard outlining the menu of what is available.

When we were kids, there were 'Christmas trees'. That was it. Christmas trees, and the only two questions to ask were: how big do you want it, and how much can we rip you off? Simple. The answer to question one was in feet not metres, and the answer to question two was about five bob.

Today, as with everything else in life, there is far too much choice. Variables include the supposed country of origin, the variety, the needles – further subdivided into the shape and any particular 'dropping' characteristics. Then there is the matter of with or without cones, and eventually the price per foot. Christmas trees are one of the few things which appear not to have gone metric; which may tell us as much about the people who sell them as it does about anything else.

'Guaranteed non-drop' is my favourite

advertising slogan. Oh well, that'll be lovely, a nice guarantee from the bloke in the high street. So then if we find that the pine needles do indeed make a mess in the car, on the carpet, all through the house on the way out, or in the front garden while we're working out how to get rid of the bloody thing, we can return to his place of business and this nice man will give us our money back. Probably.

So we have to go through this extended ritual of first of all identifying a tree which is roughly the right height – which is not as easy as it sounds for the reasons outlined above. After all, you're standing in the middle of the high street, and trying to envisage the height of your ceiling, minus the height of the stand and the height of the fairy. Tricky.

Then, and this is more difficult still, comes the question of whether it's the right shape. Making this determination is a very particular source of joy for a Grumpy Old Man who's already pissed off that he's missing the football.

'You stand there and hold it and I'll look at it, and then I'll stand and hold it while you look at it.'

So I stand there, on the pavement, always in the cold and usually in the drizzle, with my arm outstretched, while my wife cocks her head to the left and then to the right, walks around it, and decides that 'It's not quite right'.

I decline the offer to allow her to stand propping it up so that I can walk a few paces away and look at it. I know I won't have any worthwhile opinion as to the shape of the Christmas tree, and anyway at this point I'd buy a cone-shaped oak tree if it would speed up the process.

We find another one of approximately the desired height and I get to hold it up while she stands back to look at it from this angle, and then from that. Then another, and then another. I'm asked if I can manage to stand a bit further away from it, arm outstretched, so that my wife can see the whole silhouette of the tree. At this stage just a glance at the expression on my face is enough.

Eventually, one is declared to be the winner of this close-fought competition and, though he doesn't actually have a mask and a gun, the man selling the trees might as well have. It's as close as you're likely to get to being mugged in broad daylight. And, of course, the astronomical price you've paid doesn't include anything as helpful as delivery, so how are we going to get this mighty tree back home?

Well, in some cases the same GOM mentality that has briefly envisaged the life of a lumberjack was also at play when it was decided to buy a 4 x 4. This is one of the total of two occasions in the year when the purchase of the semi-military heavy-duty service vehicle in which you usually just commute from Putney to Victoria can be said to have a point. (The other is the one day a year when the snows fall heavily enough to lie on the ground for longer than twenty minutes.)

If you're one of these outdoor types with a 4 x 4, all you have to do now is to open the back doors, wish you'd remembered to clear out the accumulation of Wellingtons, anoraks, jump-leads, tool boxes, umbrellas, hats, maps and papers which has been gathering grime since this time last year, remember how to fold down the rear seats, damn nearly break your fingers in the attempt, drag the bloody Christmas tree across the pavement and then spend five more minutes deciding whether it would be easier to put it in forwards or backwards.

Eventually, you insert the tree base-first so that the clump of soil-covered root is resting against the gear lever, making it impossible to engage second or fourth, and loose earth still attached to the roots can fall liberally onto and through those little bristles that lead to the transmission and which were already covered with the crumbs from the Cornish pasty you ate in the car in October. Phew.

If you haven't got a 4 x 4 but you've got a hatchback, all the above applies, except worse. Then you wonder how you're also going to get the kids in, briefly consider suggesting that they get the bus, and eventually ask them to nestle somewhere in the gap between the front and rear seats, just so you can all get home.

If you haven't got a 4 x 4 or a hatchback, you're fucked.

In our house there are two possible places for the Christmas tree: one is in the living room, where it looks most festive and where we open the presents on Christmas morning but where, as we spend most of our time living in the kitchen, it won't be seen very much until the day itself. The other is the corner of the kitchen where we also eat. Here we would see it more often in the run-up to Christmas, but then we wouldn't be able to see it as we open our presents or watch the Queen. And, of course, we'll be taking a detour around it for a fortnight.

In earlier years, the cats solved this by finding it irresistible to climb the sodding thing and bring it down on their heads. This usually used to happen in the middle of the night so that I thought we had burglars and could never get back to sleep after I'd sent my wife downstairs to investigate. So it had to stay in the living room where the cats were not allowed to go. Now that the one remaining cat is so fat, old and lazy that she could no more climb the tree than I could, that has been eliminated as a factor.

Anyway, the point is that we have the same

debate year after year, and eventually we decide to put it in the living room, where it can moult over the only rug in the house that's worth anything, and where we can forget about looking at it until Christmas morning.

So now how are we going to stand it up? You've been through this, haven't you? You must have.

Actually – and for a Grumpy Old Man this really is a serious concession and one to treasure – I think this genuinely is one of the very few things in life that has in fact improved. I know, I know; amazing, isn't it? Nowadays we do in fact have a more-or-less foolproof device into which we clamp the tree, and which can be more or less guaranteed to hold it up. This year there was scarcely any trauma involved in this part of the process at all, but when I think back on the bloody bollocks I've been through over the years getting there...

When we were kids the operation used to involve what I recall must have been a milk bottle and a waste-paper bin made out of tin. I seem to think that my father would somehow force the bottom of the tree into the bottle, wrap wedges of rolled-up news-paper around it until it was wide enough to jam into the tin bin, and hope that would hold the thing upright. Of course the base of the tree would never go into the milk bottle, and so a variety of sharp instruments would be brought to bear, blood and blasphemies would flow in equal measure, and eventually the thing would stand upright. Precariously. Always precariously. Remembering all that suggests to me that the trees involved must have been smaller than I recall them to be, but then I guess everything is big when you are little yourself.

Over the years I've tried a lot of variations on that theme, but since we've usually had trees of a size which might otherwise have made them candidates for Trafalgar Square, this has never been a simple matter. I used to try wedging the base in between a selection of builder's bricks in a large tin bucket and filling it up with sand. But then you could never get the angle of the bricks just right, and manoeuvring them at arm's length with sharp pine needles sticking in your ears and down your neck was always an activity guaranteed to bring out the best in me; thereby ensuring that I was in the most affable of moods when it came to the tree decoration.

We've also had a variety of those green plastic devices from B&Q and other places which look like instruments of torture, are supposed to slot together and are guaranteed to keep the tree upright. One was a sort of enlarged plant-pot with wedges to drive in to hold the tree in place. Another involved long clamps that you had to screw into the base of the tree. Have any of these ever worked for you? Did you ever put the thing in position, stand back, and find it was upright? We never did.

Anyway, finally this year my wife managed to purchase a device which is sufficiently robust and heavy to support the weight of this enormous tree, with clamps that seem to grip the thing effectively. So all I had to do was to find a way to manhandle the thing into the living room, lift it off the ground for long enough to be able to kick this new-fangled base beneath it, line it up so that the base of the tree fitted into the hole, prop up the tree against the wall while I lay flat on the floor manipulating the bolts, and then make some minor adjustments. All relatively trauma-free compared to recent years.

Next comes the decorating. Now I've said many times before that grumpiness is not about age, and not even about sex, but is mostly about a state of mind. However, I suspect that evolution has determined that the core years of grumpiness are between thirty-five and fifty-four for a reason. Or maybe several reasons. In this case the reason would be that it's difficult for even the grumpiest of Grumpy Old Men to be grumpy when decorating a Christmas tree in the presence of very young children. Though it goes very much against the grain to say it, the looks on their little faces as they break out the baubles and unravel the tinsel for another year would melt the heart even of someone as terminally grumpy as I am.

We used to set the scene by putting a recording of Christmas carols on (what we used to call) the hi-fi. And that's another thing; why is it never possible to buy a record of a decent choir singing all the carols you know and grew up with as a kid, but with no esoteric madrigals in Latin that you don't know and don't care for? Anyway, it isn't, so you have to put up with some songs you don't know among the ones you can join in with.

The kids would stumble about, grabbing hold of glass baubles which threatened to shatter in their hands, standing on the fairy lights so you could hear them crunch underfoot, throwing tinsel at the tree in great clumps. Linda Robson in *Grumpy Old Women at Christmas* told how she and her husband used to let the kids decorate the tree as they liked, and then when they'd gone to bed, would take everything off the tree and start again. Isn't it marvellous how you can pull those kinds of stunts on your kids and no one ever seems to notice?

However, when you've done this a few times, and the children are beyond that first stage of innocence and gullibility, how much of a pain in the arse does it become? For example, one of the things we like to think distinguishes us as humans from most of the animal kingdom is that we learn from our mistakes. So why has the tinsel always been tied together like Bob Marley's dreadlocks? Why don't we know which of the six brown cardboard boxes with 'tree decorations' scrawled on the side contains the paper lanterns that the kids made in Miss Peat's class at school? And why oh why didn't we check all the bulbs before we wrapped a string of about 100 of them around the tree?

Has any set of lights that you used last year ever worked first time when you plug it in this year? Not in our house it hasn't. And so it begins: you start at the one nearest to the plug and give every bulb a little push (expecting it to break in your fingers every time), and a little twist (expecting it to come off in your hand) and hoping against hope that something you're doing is magically going to illuminate the whole lot. It doesn't, and so now you're looking for that tiny little polythene bag which you seem to remember contained two spare bulbs for this set of lights. Or were they for the other set of lights that we put round the mirror?

Anyway it doesn't matter because you can't find them, or maybe you can find them, but you do so by stepping back on them. It's all going rather well, don't you think?

There's no alternative but to get your coat on, get the car out, and join the queues for the car park at Woolies or Homebase or wherever the hell to get another set. You feel like asking, 'Do you have a set that costs ten times what these sets cost, but which has a chance of lasting for more than one year?', but that would be a waste of time. So you buy two more sets of crappy lights, ask if they sell spare bulbs separately, which, of course, they wouldn't dream of doing, and within an hour or two you're back joining in the fun. Smelling of alcohol.

After about six hours and most of the seasonal goodwill in your family has evaporated in the process, the fairy is ceremonially stuck on top of the tree and everything is finally ready. We close the curtains, stand back, switch on the tree lights and collectively go 'aaah'. Then we look at each other and wonder what next.

And the only thing worse than that – the only thing more of a waste of time with less in the way of reward – is taking it down. Oooh, the joys we still have to come ... eh?

8

The Nativity Play

One of the pleasures of being a Grumpy Old Man, if that doesn't seem like too much of a contradiction in terms, is that we're at the stage in our lives when we can call things exactly what they are. To use one of those irritating Americanisms which, in this case, sums it up nicely – you can 'call it like you see it'.

Many of our GOMs have reflected upon this eloquently. When you're young, you think carefully about what you are going to say and wonder about the effect it will have on other people and what they will think of you. 'Is this a cool thing to say?' 'Does this seem an OK attitude to have?' 'Will my views chime in with those of my mates?' 'How will this affect my career?' 'Will this improve my chances of getting laid?' etc., etc.

But the joy of getting to thirty-five, forty or forty-five, or whatever age the onset of grumpiness arrived for you, is that you start to not give a damn. You'll see something stupid, or ridiculous (a sub-set of stupid), or unattractive or unpleasant, and you'll say so; without worrying too much what others think about it. Or about you for what you've said. Naturally this behaviour can quite often cause offence to others around you, but equally I've found that it can just as easily break the ice.

Since I've started doing it, and have called things what they are as opposed to what is socially acceptable, as often as not I've found that everyone else is relieved, and that all the while others have been secretly thinking very much the same thing. You might be standing around in a small group at a wedding reception, and someone will say what a lovely service it was. One by one, all round the group everyone will agree – but often with diminishing degrees of conviction. When it comes to me I'll say: 'Actually I thought it was shitty. The church was cold, the choir was on drugs, the groom looked a bit uncertain and the vicar could hardly remember his own name, let alone the names of the bride and groom.'

Sometimes you'll see people stiffen up – especially if one of the group is the bride's sister – but as often as not everyone will relax and one of them will say, 'And what about the bridesmaids? I couldn't tell the difference between their dresses and the wedding cake.' And then someone else will make their little contribution and before you know it everyone is coming out with

109

what they really thought. 'I know – what did she think she looked like?'

You should try it; it can be very liberating.

All of which is a long way round to commenting on what happened when Bob Geldof made his remarks in the first series of *Grumpy Old Men* about school plays. 'School plays,' he intoned in his unmistakable and if I may say so quintessential Grumpy Old Man voice, 'are total complete and utter shite.' He went on equally poetically to describe having to turn up and to sit for hours and hours through seemingly endless lamentable performances, when you'd much rather be at home watching the telly.

When he said that, I don't know about you, but I think I felt a nationwide exhalation of relief. The end of the mutually agreed conspiracy in which every parent of every child in every school had silently agreed to pretend that school plays and nativity plays are lovely, and that there is nothing we'd rather do on a cold wintry night than to go to see one. Actually, almost all of us hate school plays of any kind, and the only people who like going to see them are a few mums who can't help but start to weep upon hearing the words 'nativity play' let alone attending one.

But school nativity plays, like everything else, are a whole lot different today from when Grumpy Old Men were kids. Indeed, it's not easy to imagine, is it, what children

110

these days must make of the whole business of the birth of Jesus.

When we were young (there it is, a phrase I think I've managed to avoid up to this point; I don't know what page we're on, but I don't think that's bad going), when we were young, it was all quite magical. We didn't have to wait until Christmas to know who Jesus was because we used to start our day, every day, with a morning assembly of the whole junior school in which we would sing some hymns and say some prayers.

The hymns would be accompanied by Miss Woodburn on the upright piano in the corner of the school hall, and for the prayers we would have to keep our eyes tightly shut and our hands pressed together, fingers pointing upwards, in front of us. I'm not sure that I ever knew why we had to keep our eyes closed; you'd have thought it would be something worth explaining to a six-year-old, wouldn't you? We just knew that they had to remain tightly closed, on pain of going straight to hell, even if someone next to you was larking about. Not an easy task.

Then there would be a little 'thought for the day' of some sort from the headmaster, Mr Spanner. In it there was always an underlying message about kindness, or consideration, or manners, or respect for teachers or some other undoubtedly Christian virtue. Mr Spanner was a terrifying bloke who always wore a pin-stripe suit and had terrible halitosis – except that aged six I didn't realise it was halitosis but just thought of it as being breath that threatened to make you bring up your school lunch on the spot.

One of the many reasons to avoid bad behaviour in those days was that if you got told off, Mr Spanner would stand very close to you and breathe his horrid breath directly into your face, with potentially terrible consequences. Mr Spanner was probably about thirty but seemed from my perspective to be about seventy and you made it your business to listen hard to whatever he said because if you didn't, in addition to the imminent danger of projectile vomiting into his handkerchief pocket, he'd cuff you across the top of the head with a board rubber.

Aside from the generous gospel according to Mr Spanner, we also had the benefit of regular Bible study with our class teacher, Miss Tresize. Again, I certainly didn't realise it at the time, but now I think back on it, I imagine that Miss Tresize was what these days we might call a 'babe'. I remember her wearing long flared skirts that I later came to associate with Olivia Newton-John, and have a vivid image of her swishing along the corridor, closely followed by the gym teacher whose name I can't remember and who certainly didn't look much like John Travolta but who no doubt had very much the same intent.

Anyway, Bible study. Do you remember all those wonderful books with fabulous illustrations? Stories like the feeding of the 5,000 (a subject we'll return to when we come to modern Christmas food shopping. It's like the feeding of the 5,000, except that we take enough food to feed 5,000 but use it to feed just five).

Or the water into wine? A very good trick if you can pull it off, that one, but one which I never thought of as being entirely Christian. Zaccheus climbing the sycamore tree; Jesus riding a donkey down the hill to the adulation of the crowds. Didn't he look cool? Long flowing hair in a style we'd all be emulating in a few years. Benign expression. Rays of sunshine bursting through from heaven and bathing the scene in glorious black and white. All that worship and walking on water.

Oh yes, we knew the Bible stories all right.

There were two Jewish kids in our class at Gipsy Hill Junior School, and I remember them being excused assembly. They didn't seem to mind and we didn't seem to mind either, and no one said anything about it one way or the other. There were no Muslims, Hindus, Buddhists or Scientologists. No atheists or Jains, and hardly even a Methodist. And while we're on the subject, we may as well record that every kid was

113

white and every kid had two parents living together in the same house.

What point am I trying to make? None at all just for the moment, thank you, other than that those were very different times, and that in those very different times there was no controversy about Christmas. It was when our Lord Jesus Christ was born, and boy were we going to celebrate the hell out of it. Except that obviously we didn't say 'celebrate the hell' in those days, and probably – my wife points out – very few of us say it now.

As if all that good stuff at junior school wasn't enough, we also went to Sunday school at the local church. Again, looking back on it, my parents were not especially religious and probably regarded this as a sort of free crèche which would get us out of the house and allow them what might have been the only bit of peace they got in the whole week. Now I think about it, I seem to recall wondering why the beds weren't made by the time we got home.

But the point is that at Sunday school, with Christmas on the horizon, we got the whole magical story year after year. It was not explained to us as 'one theory', not delivered as 'some people believe', not as any kind of allegory, but as the gospel truth. There were three wise men, right? Three shepherds watching their flocks in the fields

114

by night all seated on the ground, when the angel of the Lord came down and glory shone around. OK? We believed it all. It all happened just like they said it did.

I'm not claiming that we were above a little light satire, but I think even then there was a frisson of blasphemy when we sang 'While shepherds washed their socks by night all seated round the tub, a bar of angel soap came down and they all began to scrub.' Do you know what I mean? If one of us had been struck down by a thunderbolt at that moment, it would obviously have been a shock for the person thus smitten, but I'm not sure that the rest of us would have been all that amazed. Probably we had it coming.

So anyway, nativity plays. As far as we were concerned, all we were doing was re-enacting something that had actually happened. It was a kick. God knows it's all a very long time ago but if I torture my brain sufficiently mercilessly, I think I can still recall the thrill of being told I was going to be one of the three shepherds one year, and running home to tell my mum and dad. I had a few lines to learn – rather fewer, on mature reflection, than this starring role ought to have merited – but best of all I got to wear my dressing gown and a tea-towel wrapped round my head and tied up with a bit of cord. And my holiday sandals.

Wendy Simmons was Mary, and it's not just the rosy hue of remembrance of things past that gives me the retrospective hots for her. To this day I have a photograph of Wendy Simmons and me aged about nine with our arms round each other. She looks fabulous and I look a dweeb: I wonder whatever happened to Wendy? If by any chance you're reading this now, Wendy, why not...? Oh I don't know; probably better not.

My theatrical debut was not recorded for any possible eventual appearance on *This Is Your Life* because obviously those were the days before video cameras, and although we did have a rather swish Kodak 127 (which indeed I still have), it was certainly not capable of taking pictures indoors. A camera with a flash was still a long way out of our reach.

Anyway, it was great. We got to perform the play once in the afternoon, and once in the evening. But here's the best thing about it: I guess it probably lasted about forty minutes, end to end, with a number of musical interludes. Every parent of every child came to see it, they all sat in their seats looking proud, and after the evening performance we got to stop up late and had orange juice and little cakes. Well, you had to make your own entertainment in those days.

So what's it like today?

Well, it has to be said that the good thing

is that life is much more interesting. Where once we had a lot of stuffy old Christian tradition all painted in a bland white emulsion, now we've got a vivid multicoloured array of different backgrounds, cultures, beliefs and perspectives. The class is full of kids whose parents come from all parts of the world, have brought with them entirely different traditions and value-systems, and in most ways it's all so much the better for that. All much more fun and so much more interesting than those monochromatic days. That's the good bit.

The bad bit is that it's brought with it a load more opportunities for the usual brigade of interfering, patronising, holier-than-thou bureaucratic wankers who want to police every aspect of our lives and stick their horrid blackhead-ridden snozzes into our business. You know the species. Shitty little local councillors with their nasty little minds and horrible little rules who can't leave things alone and just have to bloody well interfere.

So we find that we can't celebrate Christmas, but have to give equal weight to Diwali or Eid or Hanukkah, or whatever it is. That a parent can't dress up as Santa because that's giving undue prominence to one culture over the others, who might therefore feel left out. That the three wise men must be referred to as the three wise persons and

that Bing needs to be dreaming of a multicoloured Christmas. That Christmas cards
aren't allowed to refer to Christ but have to
say 'happy holidays' or some other cop-out.
All godsends for the headline writers of the
Daily Redneck or any of the range of other
reactionary rags that feed off all this total
bollocks and never fail to take the opportunity to bore all the rest of us to death.

For the sake of entertainment, I'd like to be
able to report that all this political correct-
ness blighted the Christmas experience of
Matt and Lizzie when they were at school,
but for one reason or another, it didn't. In
this respect we were reasonably fortunate.
No, the experience of their nativity plays was
blighted by something else – the more
modern scourge of digital bloody cameras.

My first direct experience of this new
pestilence actually involved Matt and Lizzie
and their appearance in the school play. I
am reluctant to record it, because after *The
Secret Diary* both kids said they would leave
home if I retailed any more details of their
private lives. Obviously, I don't regard that
in itself as any kind of threat – neither of
them can afford to leave home – and like I'd
care anyway. However, in this case even I
have been wondering if the story may be too
close to home to relate.

So being a man of principle, what I've
decided to do is to put it down here, and if

in the end the word-count of the book is too high, we'll take it out. If you're reading it, you can assume we were a bit short.

The story is that, for reasons I won't bore you with, our kids went to the same school as several of the younger kids of Mick Jagger and Jerry Hall. All credit to them for sending their kids to a relatively ordinary local school. It always caused a bit of a stir among the other mums when Jerry dropped them off, which she did fairly regularly. Anyway that's not the point. The point is that one year the kids were doing the Christmas play, and one of the Jagger kids was in it and so was Lizzie.

Loads of parents turned up early to secure seats that would give them a clear line of sight; many of them had the usual clunky video cameras and all that stuff. Then, just as the performance was about to start, who should walk in wearing a coat and scarf which looked as if they must have been borrowed from Dr Who, but Mick Jagger?

Consternation among the teachers. Obviously they hadn't known that he was coming, and there is nowhere for him to sit where he can get a decent view. After all, he's late for Christ's sake. All the seats are taken by parents who turned up early, and although several of them are also rather thrilled that Mick is here, none looks ready to give up their seat for him. Even if they were inclined to do so, it would look terribly creepy.

Anyway, the risk of looking terribly creepy didn't worry the teachers. One of them, and I won't say who because that probably is too close to home, leapt to his feet and ushered Mick to this favoured position like he was the bloody Dalai Lama. I mean it; you've never seen anything so retch-inducing in your whole life. If Nelson Mandela had walked in, he wouldn't have been treated with any more awe.

Eventually the thing gets under way. I suppose it's sort of cute in a 'my kid is in it' sort of way, and that would have been the end of the story except that it seems that Mick has brought his own tiny little camera, far smaller and obviously more groovy than anything anyone else had, and then proceeds to shoot the proceedings like he is Fellini.

He's getting up out of his seat and moving over here to the left to get a better shot from this angle; he's standing up to get a high shot; he's leaning across the people next to him to get that shot where everyone else's head silhouettes the action. Oh yes, it's the school sodding nativity play and he's remaking *Performance*. And I don't think I heard anyone whispering to *him* to sit down. Indeed, I suspect that Mick himself appears as an extended cutaway-shot in just about every other home video of the bloody evening.

So maybe not much of an anecdote, except that it was my first direct experience of the sort of thing that now totally obliterates any pleasure that anyone might ever have had in going to see a performance at a school. The other bloody parents.

Over the years it has become worse and worse and worse, so that nowadays it seems like every idiot father thinks he is the first person anywhere in the world to have children, and every utterance, facial expression and fart brought forth by his offspring has to be recorded with the most expensive and hi-tech photographic equipment that money can buy. Competition for which part your kid is going to play is matched only by the size and expense of the outside broadcast unit with full lighting rig you want to bring to the school to record it.

So let's be clear: even in the old days before the world went digital, going to any performance of any sort at your kids' school was an absolutely almighty pain in the tush. Let's admit it, it was. Your child has insisted that you get there at the start because 'all the Mums and Dads are', and when you get the programme the piece they are performing in isn't even on the first three pages. Then sitting on hard seats for hours on end in draughty school halls, waiting through decades of crappy performances by out-of-tune adolescents, one after another, until

121

you thought they would never end. At last, after half of your total allotted time-span on earth has elapsed, the piece your kid is appearing in at last hoves onto the horizon, and they decide that this would be a good moment for an interval. Everyone breaks up, rushes for a cup of tea or, horror of horrors, a polystyrene cup of warm white wine, and exchanges small-talk with other parents or teachers about what a wonderful performance it is.

Eventually, just as you have lost all hope of ever regaining any feeling from your waist down, your kid pops up. You sit there beaming encouragement, wanting to catch their eye but hoping against hope that in doing so you don't distract them so they forget what they have to do. If you're honest you'd have to say that the performance was at best indifferent and at worst excruciating, and you start to formulate in your mind the words you're going to say that will impart unambiguous praise and encouragement but not be a total lie. Maybe 'lovely' or 'remarkable'. Well, they're your kids – what are you going to do?

Ideally you'd like nothing better on earth than to be able to bolt for the exit, but if all that wasn't bad enough, there are eight more performances after your kid's turn, and just as the applause dies down and you're headed for the playground to get your car, the headmaster appears on the stage looking unctuous.

Has anyone in the history of schooling ever been to one of these performances which wasn't the best the headmaster had ever seen? Has anyone ever been to one where the school wasn't extraordinarily lucky to have on its staff someone as talented as the music teacher, or someone as dedicated as Miss Farmer from 3B? Has anyone ever been to one where they don't feel a wave of nausea overtake them as the teachers put on that 'it was nothing' face which really means they hope they'll get promotion to deputy head next year? For heaven's sake.

No, as in quite a few other things, most Grumpy Old Men subjected to yet another 'entertainment' at the school find themselves agreeing with the poetic erudition of Bob Geldof on the subject: 'School plays are uniformly shite.'

9

The Panto

Well, this may be as good a time as any to admit something which you may, perhaps, have half suspected. What might that be? Well, it's this: it's not completely unknown for Grumpy Old Men to exaggerate. Just slightly. Sometimes, for the sake of what we obviously vainly hope is entertainment, what comes out of our mouths is just a little bit more extreme than what we are really feeling.

So that for example, when I say I'd rather have a nine-foot-long skewer stuffed up my arse and be roasted on a spit and eaten by an army of Amish than to go to Jeremy and Emily's barbecue, the real truth is that if in any currently unforeseeable circumstances I was really given that actual choice, I'd probably go to the barbecue. So long as it wasn't going to last more than about twenty minutes or so.

Or when I say that if I see one more over-weight, spotty tuneless geek bursting into tears when some smug git on the telly tells him that his pet monkey has more talent in its foreskin than the kid has in his entire body, I'll feed the TV into the shredder, I probably don't mean it. The shredder isn't anything like big or robust enough.

However, if you doubt what I'm about to write about Christmas pantos, feel free to ask my kids.

On the day that I am sitting in a little wicker chair with a tartan rug over my knees, staring out to sea, and someone suggests that I might like to go to see that panto, please switch me off. Yes, that's right, I really mean it. That's the time to flick the switch and let's call it a day.

I've gone on and on about this so much over the years that nowadays Matt and Lizzie know better than to comment. However, at one time, Lizzie in particular was a bit more sensitive about this sort of thing and sometimes would respond with something warm and caring like 'I don't think I could actually flick the switch'. When that happened, I'd smile at her as though this was a wonderful sign of affection, and just reply that she didn't actually have to do anything; she should just leave the tablets and a glass of water within easy reach when she left for the night. I'd take care of the rest. Or maybe just leave the hair-dryer plugged in next to my bath. Or go off and have a cup of tea leaving me and my bath-chair within a rheumatic lunge of the top of the stairs.

Actually, my instructions on this matter

have become such a commonplace in my household that the expression 'When that happens, it's panto-time' is commonly understood to mean the signal for my exit. Stage left.

So how, you may be asking, did this arise? (And if you're not, this might be a good moment to skip on to the next chapter.) It started about twenty years ago when, for some extraordinary reason that I'm now quite unable to recall, I was prevailed upon to take Matt and Lizzie to the panto. By that I don't mean that I don't think they should have gone to the panto; in principle I had no objection to the panto and was perfectly happy that they should go. What is amazing is that on this occasion I should have been the one to take them.

Careful readers might by now be getting at least a sketchy understanding of the division of responsibilities in the Grumpy household. None of it is written down, or even acknowledged in any official sort of way. And indeed, there are some areas of ambiguity and overlap.

One example in this latter category is changing the loo roll. Years ago it was commonly understood that something like changing the loo roll would be my wife's task. However, over the years it has become one of those totemic things, and cute phrases like 'the loo-roll fairy' have crept into our household vocabulary – carrying with them the clear implication that it is every bit as easy for the person who uses the last of the existing loo roll to replace it, as it is for the loo-roll fairy on whom we all seem to rely. So now, in such instances, I take my turn. I even shape the first sheet into a little paper dart as they do in hotels – just to let everyone know that I've done it. Matt and Lizzie still don't make any effort of course, but as my wife has told them about it only around 136 times each, we wouldn't expect them to get it quite yet.

On any interpretation of the division of labour, organising a trip to the panto and taking the kids would fall unambiguously into my wife's bailiwick. So something very strange must have happened on this occasion and to my own amazement I found myself queuing to get into the Stockport Empire, or wherever it was, for a matinée of *Aladdin*. The place was packed with kids who were far too young to be at an event like this, and who were shortly going to have the crap scared out of them by Ebenezer or whatever he was called. However, with about five minutes to go to the start, I was surprised to see that the front two rows of the stalls were empty.

I didn't think much about it, other than that if the seats were still empty in a couple of minutes and the huge fat and sweaty oaf sitting in front of Matt and blocking his view was still fat, sweaty and oafish, we might move and sit at the front. The three-minute warning bell sounded and I was about to whisk the kids out of their seats, when I looked up to see a long procession coming down the aisles. I looked once, and then I looked twice, and bugger me if it wasn't an outing from the old people's home.

Now I don't want to be too supercilious about this, because one day I might be old; or you might have parents who are already old, and I don't want to disrespect anybody. But honestly. Somehow the idea of taking a group of ninety-year-olds – who knows, probably against their will – to an entertainment which frankly is a bit patronising for a child over the age of eight seems to me to be just about the bloody end.

So – and I know this doesn't reflect well on me but we're well past that point – I remember turning to the kids and saying something like 'When you are my age, and I am their age, if anyone ever suggests taking me to the panto, that's the time to switch me off'. And it's passed into family folklore. 'It's panto-time' means it's time to switch Dad off.

I hate to have to say it, but you know it's true. The panto is yet another thing that was better when you were a kid than it usually is now. We might feel this way because we were kids then and far more easily impressed than we are now that we are jaundiced old sods whose idea of a good time is just being left the hell alone. However, I think it is objectively true.

The late great John Peel reflected on this when we made our *Grumpy Old Men at Christmas* programme for BBC2. He remembered going to the panto and watching wonderful comic actors like Frankie Howerd or Jimmy Jewel. Or you might see the fabulous Arthur Askey, or Sid James or Kenneth Williams. Proper comic actors or genuinely funny people with stage skills and some idea of what a panto is supposed to be.

Who is it now?

Well, without turning this into an academic thesis on modern-day interpretations of the *commedia del'arte*, it seems to me as I scan through the theatre listings that there are four categories of people appearing in panto these days.

First, and probably the least explicable, there seems to be a fashion for proper actors – you know, real thesps like Ian McKellen and Kevin Spacey – to suddenly want to frock up outrageously in a lot of hoops and girdles and tread the boards. I'm not going to comment on the coincidence of these blokes' sexual preference because that's crass and we're not writing that sort of book. Suffice it to say that it seems to me to be a relatively new phenomenon and one which I'd be surprised to see as more than a passing fad.

The second group is all right – I suppose

they're the inheritors of the Sid James and Arthur Askey tradition. I'm talking about people like Matthew Kelly or probably even Jimmy Tarbuck, if he's still doing that sort of thing. Almighty twits, but inoffensive enough by and large, and probably right in their metier at the panto.

However, there is a third category, and perhaps the best way of describing them is that they used to be the part-time weather presenter from Border Television. Or they read the sports results on a Saturday afternoon on Grampian. Indeed, they might be anyone else who has ever appeared on television in any capacity. For some reason, even in our dark and cynical times, there remains a strange and inexplicable interest in, and fascination for, people who are sometimes on the telly.

I know this from personal experience. About 120 years ago I was a TV news reporter and used to appear regularly on a programme broadcast by BBC North East called *Look North*. I wasn't any good, and no one would have known me from Adam except that this job involved me in sitting next to a bloke who was, and is, a household name throughout the region – the legendary Mike Neville. Mike is a genuine phenomenon; I think he is mentioned in the *Guinness Book of Records* as the longest-serving anchor of any nightly news magazine anywhere in the world. But even then, way back in the last century, he was a huge favourite.

Anyway, because everyone tuned in to see Mike, for a while they also saw me, and so just a little bit of his undoubted stardust rubbed off. And believe it or not, as a callow and untutored youth, I occasionally used to be asked to do what I believe are called 'personal appearances'.

Modesty and embarrassment have probably filtered out most of any escapades of this kind from my memory. However, a hand-made commemorative mug on one of my bookshelves bears witness to the occasion when I travelled after work up to Berwick for the annual festival to crown the Berwick Salmon Queen. And quite an honour it was, too. I also did once host an entirely spectacular evening of entertainment in Blyth – the Atlantic City, New Jersey of the north-east – at which the star of the show was none other than the wonderful Dickie Henderson. Remember him? Maybe not, but I do, and actually he was rather good.

Best for all concerned to draw a discreet veil over these events and I include them only because otherwise, as I'm taking the piss out of their modern-day equivalents, someone is bound to expose me as a hypocrite. Sort of like David Cameron condemning drug use but admitting that he smoked a bit of dope. If he did. Or whatever.

Anyway the point is that in towns and villages up and down the country, the star of the panto is the bloke who does the 'what's on' round-up on the telly on a Thursday evening and whose drink habit requires him to earn a bit of extra money at Christmas. Or the woman you usually see standing outside the Town Hall trying to interview the pickets when the local dustmen or teachers are threatening to strike. All famous enough, apparently, to draw into the theatre in the high street anyone whose lives would be made complete by seeing their local celebrity dressed in tights and making a prat of themselves.

Actually a sub-section of this category which is well deserving of a dishonourable mention is the failed politician or total washout comedian, for whom panto somehow seems to represent a desperate possible lifeline back to respectability. I'm thinking of people like those total toss-pots from Knutsford or wherever. The Hamiltons, is it? I believe I saw that one or other of them, or maybe both, appeared in a panto once. Can you imagine anything worse? Two total plonkers, famous for five minutes because the old man was disgraced. What a disgrace.

Which brings us to the fourth and final category – the group of those who are famous for being related to someone who is famous.

It should be said that there is, of course, a long and widely celebrated tradition of people being famous for being related to politicians. One thinks of Jimmy Carter's half-wit brother Billy who looked even more of a product of too much in-breeding than did the President. Or indeed there was Terry, the even-more-idiotic brother of John Major, with whom John once had a business making garden ornaments – strange to think of John Major having an idiot brother. Then there is the whole Mark Thatcher phenomenon. Least said and all that, but how on earth has that bloke got away with it?

However, I think this is probably a modern phenomenon as it applies to celebrities. Famous for being related to someone who may themselves not be very famous. One of our Grumpy Old Men thinks he remembers seeing a panto advertised as featuring none other than 'Gazza's sister'.

So that's the cast – all drawn from one of four categories, and all of them a bit weird in one way or another. But the cast is by no means the only thing about modern pantos which is lamentably worse than when we were kids. What about the scripts?

A long, long time ago, when we were small, pantos were for the kids. The show was full of silly jokes and slapstick and set at exactly the eye-level of the target audience. Loads of fun and audience participation.

133

You'd get home exhausted, with a sore throat, and with a good feeling about going to the theatre which might have a chance of lasting into adulthood.

In those days parents were happy to take the kids to the panto just because it was great to see them all having a terrific time. By and large you had to make your own entertainment in those days – no Segas or Megas or Lara Crofts (more's the pity) – and therefore a really good afternoon out when the kids would do nothing but shout and laugh was a treat all round.

Then maybe, who knows, perhaps in more cynical days the panto started to lose its popularity and appeal. Audiences were dwindling, and no doubt someone said that a way had to be found to make it entertaining for the adults as well as for the kids. 'Perhaps it can work on two levels,' said this imaginary smart-alec. 'Let's write it so that we keep all the slapstick and shouting for the kids, but also put in a layer of humour that will go over their heads but which the parents will get.'

And so it came to pass. All of a sudden – before it was OK even in show business to be overtly gay – casts were full of John Inman-type characters for whom the phrase 'He's behind you' carried a whole different meaning. Suddenly the massive bosoms and bums which padded out the Ugly Sisters were being pushed up and out or pushed back in. What had just been a ridiculous part of the costume became a source of giggling innuendo. Lots of 'oops dearie' and saucy seaside-postcard humour.

Well now – what do we imagine? Did that work, do you think? Have you ever heard an adult come out of a pantomime and say, 'I thought that Widow Twanky worked very well on two levels. While the kids obviously very much enjoyed the traditional panto-mime humour, my wife and I greatly appre-ciated the wit and repartee which worked on an altogether different plane'? No? I didn't think so. What you've heard is a lot of parents saying, 'What on earth was that embarrassing shit? Why can't they just get on and entertain the kids and leave the puerile smut at home?' Sounds a bit more like it, doesn't it?

So back to the Stockport Empire and my little trip with the kids to see *Aladdin*. Need-less to say the gentle folk from the old people's home enjoyed themselves enor-mously, despite the fact that several looked a bit bewildered and others needed so many visits to the conveniences that it's a good job they probably already knew the plot. Only one delightful old chap looked miserable throughout, and eventually fell asleep, pro-ceeding to snore loudly and dribble copi-ously down the front of his shirt. That, I felt certain, would be me in similar circum-

135

stances. Thereby further confirming my feeling that the best thing to do would be to switch me off.

Like everything else about Christmas, the panto used to be fun, and now with very few exceptions it's shit. Anyone want to disagree with that? No? I didn't think so.

10

Christmas Number Ones

What sort of music is going to be playing at the moment you die? Is that something you ever wonder about? I do. As I'm getting older, as well as getting grumpier, I've started to think about this sort of thing quite a lot. It's a sign of advancing years.

For the last few years I've been carrying a list of eight pieces around with me just in case the guest on *Desert Island Discs* should suddenly be taken poorly and I happen to be passing their office just as they decide that this week might be the opportunity to give a chance to a nobody with a book to plug – for a change.

I've also thought about what recordings should be played at my funeral, and have imparted the list in detail to my wife. However, she is so sentimental that every time I ask her to repeat it back to me, she can't remember a single one.

Lately I've been thinking about what sort of music would I like to be playing when I die? Given a choice I might want to be listening to one of the anthems of my life: maybe Dylan playing 'Subterranean Homesick Blues' or Clapton singing 'Nobody Knows You when You Are Down and Out'. In another mood, when I'm feeling ever so slightly more refined, I think it would be good to be hearing a bit of Mozart or even one of those great arias by Puccini. Sublime stuff, composed in heaven, to elevate the soul and carry it over the threshold between our earthly toils and our future in paradise.

But here's the thing. I have a sort of odd premonition that the last song I'm ever going to hear as I drift into the hereafter, with my eyes closed and my life ebbing away, is going to be Roy Wood singing 'I Wish It Could Be Christmas Every Day'.

Now just exactly how depressing a prospect is that?

I don't know where this thought came from, and I genuinely wish I'd never had it. But now that I have, I appear to be stuck with it. I don't seem to be able to banish it from my mind. It's there, and frankly it just makes me feel nauseous right down to the muesli-grouts at the bottom of my stomach.

No heavenly choirs. No lutes or harps. No angelic voices. Instead a tortured squeal torn out of the larynx of an unreconstructed refugee from the 1960s whose main redeeming feature is that the only thing that has acknowledged the passing of forty years for him is his bathroom scales.

Which is a shame in a way because about 100 years ago, when I was a teenager, I used to quite like Roy Wood. Do you remember 'The Move'? And 'Wizard' – remember? 'Fire Brigade'. Remember that one? Sing it with me: 'Get the fire brigade, get the fire brigade, see the buildings start to really burn. Uoogh!'

I know you couldn't ever take him seriously, not as a proper musician or anything, but I always used to think that the outfit was cool in a naff sort of way. And while I don't recall ever having heard him say anything, he didn't seem like a bad bloke. Also I don't suppose you can blame a chap, if he's had a hit record, from milking it a bit. After all, a person has to eat.

But honestly. Honestly! There really ought to be a limit. There really ought to be some sort of law preventing indefinite repetition, over and over and over again, year in year out, seemingly for ever. Even if it is just to safeguard the sanity of the poor fuckers working in shopping malls. And if there isn't going to be one, there ought to be some device you can employ to make sure that, whatever else happens, 'I Wish It Could Be Christmas Every Day' is not the last music you ever hear in your life. I really do think that must be something that every single one of us could agree on, don't you?

Leaving aside for a moment my own personal journey into hell and the musical accompaniment thereto, what is it, do you suppose, about Christmas music that makes it so unutterably unutterably crappy? What is the universal and apparently immutable law of nature that dictates that every song that is ever released in December for the so-called Christmas market has to be total and complete dung?

Maybe it's because all of the best music, or at least all of the best jazz, rock 'n' roll and blues, is supposed to be about depression, or rebellion or anarchy. Railing against lost love, or lost faith or against 'the man'. So that even the idea of writing an uplifting song about Christmas is doomed to be indescribably crap before the first chord is struck.

But you'd think there would be one, wouldn't you? Of all the artists over all the years who have tried to produce a distinguished record for Christmas, there would be just one that doesn't make your skin crawl so badly that it makes you want to rip it off, throw it on the floor and stamp on it.

Can you think of one? I can't. I'm by no

means an encyclopaedia of these things, but as I sit here and force my personal hard drive to engage with the question, I can't think of a single title over forty years that doesn't produce an imminent threat of throwing up my lunch.

Obviously, I don't mean to include in this a whole slew of very popular songs which maybe had been in the charts for some weeks beforehand and managed to stay there for Christmas. Songs that were nothing to do with Christmas, but just happened to be out at that time of the year. I don't mean songs like 'I Want to Hold Your Hand' by the Beatles, or 'What Do You Want to Make Those Eyes at Me For?' by Emile Ford and the Checkmates. Both fairly decent songs, in their way, which were not released for Christmas, and were not in any way about Christmas, but managed to be at number one in Christmas week.

No, I mean the songs which are cynically designed in the best Hallmark tradition as sentimental slush guaranteed to appeal to Granny at Christmas. You know the type of thing: 'Two Little Boys' by Rolf or 'Merry Christmas Everyone' by Shakin' Stevens. Fucking rubbish written, recorded and released to appeal to anyone who doesn't know what to buy for their mother at Christmas, and then destined to be trotted out on radio stations, in shopping malls, in lifts and supermarkets, every year until eternity, and then possibly be playing as you shuffle off this mortal coil.

OK, OK, so maybe I'm just jaundiced. Maybe, as I'm a Grumpy Old Man, my mind has filtered out some of the wonderful songs that have accompanied us everywhere we have gone in the weeks up to Christmas, and those joyous days trudging around the January sales. Let's go to the formal record and check my memory. Maybe I'm being unfair, and we'll find that there are some wonderful songs in the Christmas canon.

So accompany me, dear reader, to Google and enter the search words 'Christmas Number One Singles'. What do we find?

The first thing we find is that Google has located 40,000,000 results under that heading in 0.24 seconds, and is offering us numbers 1–10 on the first screen. How on earth can that be? How on earth can it be possible that there are 40 million places on the worldwide web which contain a reference to Christmas Number One Singles?

I don't mean 40 million sites referring to 'Christmas', which in itself would seem to me to be a stretch. I don't mean 40 million sites referring to 'singles', which wouldn't surprise me at all as the main preoccupation of the worldwide web is sex. But 40 million sites with a reference to Christmas Number One Singles? There, in that single fact, you have a savage indictment of the decadence of our modern society. Haven't we all got something better to do, for Christ's sake? Apparently not.

Let's check my memory against the official record. We find that we don't need 40 million sites. The very first one we click on has all the information we need. It gives the name of the record that was number one in the charts in Christmas week, in every week since 1945. That should suffice to cover the conscious experience of even the oldest of our grumpies (and anyway is, I believe, the start of what we understand as the charts).

In 1945, for example, believe it or not, the number one record was by someone with the curiously modern name of Issy Bonn. It was a tune called 'I'm in Love with Two Sweethearts'. The fact that this record doesn't sound very festive suggests that this may have been before the 'Christmas Number One Single' lunacy took hold, and the fact that no one can hum it confirms that those were the days before anything in the charts on 25 December was destined to haunt you for the rest of your life.

No, to locate one of those we have to skip past songs like 'Five Minutes More', which was at number one in 1946 and must be the only song ever sung by Frank Sinatra that I can't immediately call to mind. And we have to fly past 'An Apple-Blossom Wedding' by

Lou Praeger and Jimmy Leach which was at number one in 1947, which I don't think I've ever heard.

Indeed, we have to wait until 1948 to find the first of them. The first example of complete and utter schlock, a record with no musical or lyrical merit whatsoever, written and released for purely commercial exploitation at Christmas. Want to know what it is? Can you guess? OK, OK, let's put you out of your misery. It's 'Rudolph the Red-Nosed Reindeer' by none other than... Can you remember...? Gene Autry and Bing Crosby. Remember him? Gene Autry? Yes, you do. The Lone Ranger. 'Hiyo, Silver', Tonto and all that masked man stuff. Blimey! What a year that must have been.

Then to get to the next one we have to gallop through 'Let's Have Another Party' by Winifred Atwell, which was number one in 1954, and 'Christmas Alphabet' by the one and only Dickie Valentine in 1955, neither of which has managed to wheedle its way into my personal mental filing system.

We could turn this into an almanac of the popular music charts, but instead let's cut out the middle man and go straight to the most offensive examples of Christmas number one singles. As I glance down the list, I find myself sufficiently surprised by one or two things that I can't resist the temptation to give you a small quiz.

OK? Ready?

Question 1: in what year would you guess those lovable rascals of Slade recorded 'Merry Christmas Everyone'? Well, no sooner is the question asked than the limitations of this quiz appear obvious: this is a book and not an interactive website, so playing a guessing game can have only limited appeal. Let's just tell you that it was 1973, which seems remarkable to me because I would have said it was much later. I was still generally enjoying pop music in 1973, and I'm sure I would have spent an enormous amount of time reaching for the sick-bag if Slade had been on when I turned on the telly. Never mind; facts are facts.

OK, question 2: how many times, and with which songs, has Cliff been at number one at Christmas? Now again, left to myself, I would have said that the answer must be about seven times. Indeed, I thought there was a law that Cliff had to have a Christmas number one at least once every decade, throughout his career, which is well known to have lasted seventy years. Seventy years of show business, so you'd expect him to have had at least seven Christmas number ones. In fact the answer is a pitiful two. Just twice. With 'Mistletoe and Wine' and 'Saviour's Child'. Even the idiot Spice Girls have had more Christmas number ones than Cliff.

Finally, because this is wearing a bit thin,

the last quiz question: what is the very worst record from this list of Christmas number ones?

(A) 'Ernie, the Fastest Milk-Float in the West' by Benny Hill

(B) 'Lonely This Christmas' by Mud

(C) 'Mary's Boy Child – Oh My Lord' by Boney M

(D) 'There's No One Quite Like Grandma' by St Winifred's School Choir

(E) 'Do They Know It's Christmas?' by Band Aid

(F) 'Merry Christmas Everyone' by Shakin' Stevens

(G) 'Mr Blobby' by Mr Blobby

(H) 'Mistletoe and Wine' by Cliff Richard

Blimey. When you read them off like that, it's a much harder question than I had realised. I mean, how do you distinguish between 'There's No One Quite Like Grandma' and 'Mr Blobby'? How can you put an Esmeralda paper (remember them?) between 'Lonely This Christmas' and 'Mistletoe and Wine'? I'll leave it to you – maybe you can have a little discussion around the table on Boxing Day.

Anyway, the worst thing about Christmas music is that it's awful, and the second worst thing about it is that there seems to be no getting away from it in the weeks leading up to Christmas. Because of course there's awful music all the time, produced by hundreds and hundreds of snot-ridden bands in their dads' garages or whatever, but the important thing about it is that usually you can avoid it. (Unless it's that ponce James whatever his name is whining 'You're beautiful, you're beautiful' which, if I hear it once again, I'll be applying for a shotgun licence.) No, usually you can switch it off, or duck out of the lift at the next floor and walk up the stairs.

But there is something about Christmas music that is all pervasive. When you get out of the lift it's still playing next to the charity Christmas tree. When you walk through the precinct entrance it's playing in the walkways. When you go out of the mall, some git is playing it in the street. It's filling your head so that you think you're going to die – and, heaven help us, you're going to die to the tune of 'I Wish It Could be Christmas Every Day' by Roy Wood.

Grumpy? Can you wonder?

11

Getting the Hell Out

Regular readers will know that in our house we have reached a sort of accommodation. I am a grumpy old sod who complains about more or less everything, and my wife and family largely put up with it and go about their ordinary business as if this were not so.

So that when, for example, some impertinent idiot calls us in the evening and greets me like I'm a long-lost mate, asking me things such as have I had a nice day today, before I work out that he's trying to sell me something and tell him to sod off, they'll generally ignore me and continue with what they were talking about.

Or when the first item on the news is about something that has happened to Wayne Rooney, or Tom Cruise or David Beckham, and the second is about a lot of people dead in some part of the world they can't pronounce 'but no Britons were among the casualties', I'll usually go off on one, about modern news values, and they'll reach for the remote control to see what's on the other channels.

All very regular and routine, you might think. However, there came a time one November, about ten years ago, when my wife made some apparently casual reference to Christmas. I responded with my usual bonhomie and enthusiasm, and she – right out of the blue and rather uncharacteristically – stopped and said, 'What?'

'What do you mean, what?'

'I mean what is it this time?'

'What do you mean, what is it this time?'

'I mean, what's the problem?'

'What do you mean, what's the problem?'

I won't report all the extended preliminaries of this exchange because the fact is that it went on for some time and even I'm losing interest. So to come directly to the point, she reminded me of some of the good things about having young kids at Christmas, and asked me if I could identify exactly what it was about Christmas that made me such a miserable old fucker. (Actually, I'm pretty sure she can't have used precisely that expression, but that's how my memory recalls the scene.)

'After all,' she said, 'when you think about it, I choose and write the cards, I write the lists of stuff we need to buy, I schlep out for weeks on end to do all the present shopping and the food shopping. I do the wrapping and most of the cooking. You, on the other hand, get to stand there while the kids have

148

the best time of their lives opening the presents, and then play with them for a couple of hours before lunch. So just exactly what is there to be pissed off about in that?'

Right about now I should have smelled a rat. This was out of character. However, for some reason I was going through one of my Quasimodo phases and didn't hear any warning bells. Apparently immune to the danger signals, I blundered on.

'I don't think that's entirely fair,' I said, all the while thinking that probably it was entirely fair but I didn't really want to hear it. 'I'm sure I must do a little bit more than that? Didn't I have to go off last year and collect your Auntie Mary from the station? And unless my memory fails me, I believe it was the rush hour...' I trailed off rather lamely. Already I was running out of stuff.

'No, go on,' now she was pressing me, and this was the second point at which I should, looking back on it, have had my suspicions. 'Tell me,' she continued, 'all the things about Christmas you don't like.'

I feel sure that at this stage, somewhere deep inside in the scarcely penetrable dungeons of my consciousness, I must have known that I was making a mistake. But you know how sometimes you are aware of it, but you can't stop yourself? Like that last drink that you know is going to make the difference between a slight headache and the hangover from hell, but you knock it back anyway. Or that last word in an argument which is just too near the truth and is going to come back to haunt you for years to come. It doesn't happen to me often, but sometimes it does, and this was one of those occasions.

'Well, since you ask, I don't like having to worry if the bottle of advocaat I bought last year in case your Auntie Margery should pop in and want a snowball will still be OK to drink this year. Because although Auntie Margery did turn up last year, of course she didn't want a snowball after all, she wanted a cherry brandy. So the same bottle is still in the cupboard. I don't want to throw it out because it's unopened and I hate the idea of wasting it; on the other hand, even though I'm not that fond of your Auntie Margery, I don't want to be responsible for poisoning her.'

Well, she'd asked for it. On I went. Spade in hand. Digging energetically.

'I don't like flicking through the *Radio Times* and hoping against hope that this year for one year at least there might be something on the telly that I want to watch, at a time when the kids don't want to watch something else. I don't like having the people two doors away pop in for sherry so that we can have our annual gripe about the bin-men or the postman, or whatever other straw we can grasp to try to find something

150

in common. I don't like that odd mix of carrots and swedes which we have at Christmas lunch but never have at any other time of the year. I don't like...'

At this point I thought I saw something unusual in my wife's facial expression. But by now it was too late. I was on a roll. Warming to my theme. Only just getting started...

'It's not that I mind all that much putting up the Christmas tree, but I do hate taking it down and putting away all those bloody silly baubles year after year. I can't stand listening to bloody Roy Wood or Slade or Bing Crosby or Cliff stupid bloody Richards.' (Weird though it may seem, my wife is a big fan of Cliff and I know it irritates her when I call him Richards instead of Richard, so, needless to say, I always do.)

And it was only then, finally and unmistakably, and long after it should first have been audible to me, that the alarm bell finally sounded, like a klaxon inside my brain. I remember it all in slow motion as one does a car crash or a glass of red wine falling over onto your mother-in-law's Chinese silk rug. The look of triumph on my wife's face told me that I'd gone far enough. I'd dug down deep and right below me was the landmine. She'd been happy to stand there watching me keep digging, and now it was ready to go off.

'What?' I said, suddenly fearing the worst. 'What?'

'Well,' she started slowly, 'supposing I told you that this year I've arranged for you to have all the bits about Christmas you like – like eating enough to feed the household cavalry and watching the kids have a good time – but not have to do any of the stuff you don't like?'

How stupid am I? I like to think that these days I know better, but this was a few years ago and I was less well schooled than I am now at spotting impending disaster at 1,000 yards.

'Keep all the stuff about Christmas I like, but not to have to do any of the things I've just said? No Slade, or Cliff, or eggnog, or taking down the Christmas tree? How's that possible?'

How can I describe what happened next? It was the feeling of standing on the edge of an abyss and having someone just nudge you from behind so that you lose your balance and topple backwards. Your arms whirl around like windmills for a couple of seconds but there is nothing to grab hold of. No handrails. No parachute. No sooner have you lost the perpendicular than you are in free-fall.

'We're going to take the kids to Disneyland.'

When this book is made into a feature film, this will be one of those moments which I think I first saw in *Psycho*, when the close-up of my face stays in focus, but the director pulls focus on the background, giving the impression that I am staying still and the world I inhabit is going into warp mode. A sort of 'arghhh' moment. Watch out for it.

And so it came to pass that we all went off to Disneyland for the Christmas holidays. It turned out that the airhead parents of one of the airhead kids in Lizzie's class at school had told her about what a marvellous time they'd had the previous year and, as luck would have it, her airhead husband was a travel agent and they were doing a special package deal which included the flights, the hotels, the hire-car and admittance to several of the 'must-see' attractions for the all-in bargain price of... I don't remember how much it was, but I do recall that at the time it seemed unfeasibly inexpensive. Which in itself should have been a cause for concern. Anyway, to cut to the chase, my wife had actually booked it.

Now I have to say that this is not something that has frequently happened in our household; not before and certainly not since. But it turned out in our subsequent full and frank exchange of views that my wife was so exhausted at the prospect of listening to me gripe and moan about every aspect of Christmas in suburbia yet again this year, that her choices were either to get away and do something completely different, or to ask me to reach into the waste disposal to retrieve the washing-up mop and then turn on the switch. Thankfully, she felt she had chosen the lesser of two evils, but I gather that it had been a close call.

I'll leave aside the fact that never, ever, over the course of thirty years would I have dreamed of making a decision as important as that one without consulting her, because I know that in the area of arrangements for Christmas I'm skating on thin ice. Suffice it to say that... No, on reflection, let's just leave it at that.

Anyway the upshot was that on 20 December we found ourselves rousing a nine-year-old and a seven-year-old from their beds in the small hours of the morning to wait for the taxi that was due to take us to Heathrow airport. I say 'was due' because no taxi has ever arrived at our house on time. Not ever. Sounds like an exaggeration, doesn't it? 'Fraid not.

We've lived in the same property for ten years. It's in a road which, though admittedly not very big, is listed as clearly as anything else in the A–Z. We have a number on the door, which is fairly visible from the street, and yet no taxi driver has ever managed to find it on his own.

The usual drill is as follows: we book the taxi for about half an hour earlier than we could possibly need it because we know it's going to be late. We give the address, and then we give the address again. We try to spell the name of the street, and then we try spelling it again, but every time I've been halfway through saying 'E for echo' and 'D for delta' they reply 'Delta Road?' and I realise that I'm only making things worse.

Rather inconsiderately, the name of our road ends in the word 'Glade' which is not all that familiar, and is easily mistaken, I have discovered, for everything from 'Lane' to 'Terrace'. Because it is a small road, we usually try to give the name of the slightly larger road that leads onto it. The name of the slightly larger road inconsiderately ends in the word 'Lane' which is not similar to 'Glade' and not at all similar to 'Terrace', but can, it turns out, easily be mistaken for either.

By now they think they've got it. 'Number two, Enderby Glade.' That isn't the name of our road, in case you were wondering, but I'm not giving the real name of my road in case the taxi drivers in question should recognise it and come round and assault me. Not that they could find it, but anyway...

What usually happens then is that we call the taxi company about half an hour before the taxi is due, just to confirm that they haven't forgotten us, and that they know where we are. 'It's Mr Tribble, just off Clintonbury Rise'. Or whatever.

155

They sound rather irritated; of course they haven't forgotten us, and of course they know where we are. I don't bother to correct my own name because over the years I've learned to answer to about three million variations of what it actually is, but I take the opportunity to repeat the actual address as clearly as I can. Oh yes, they've got it now. Thanks.

The time comes when the taxi is due. Two tiny children, with bleary eyes and wrapped up to the nines – indeed swaddled –against the winter chill, are standing in the hallway next to suitcases which are bulging with every item of summer clothing they possess, wrapped round about half a ton of presents. Three minutes pass. Five minutes. The phone rings.

'Mr Primble?'

'Yes.' I know what's coming next. I could mouth it in unison with him.

'I can't find Ebury Drive. Is it off Claygate Lane?'

'It doesn't matter that you can't find Ebury Drive because we don't live in Ebury Drive. We live in...' and I go into the same stuff again. I repeat the address and spell it out using the clearest diction I know how to use. I think that by now maybe he's got it, and then just a split second before he hangs up I hear him say, 'I've got it, Clingsbury Rise.' Or whatever. Click.

Now I'm wondering whether to call the cab company to point out the mistake, but then I know the phone will be engaged when he realises he's got it wrong and calls me back, and so I stand and wait by the receiver. By now twenty of the thirty minutes' leeway we had allowed have gone by, and the kids are getting fractious in the hallway. I'm wondering, as I always do at this stage, if even now I can bundle everybody and everything in the car, drive to the airport, leave everyone at departures while I go to find the long-term car park, and still make check-in at a time when they won't tut tut and split us up to the four corners of the plane. The phone rings.

'Mr Preamble?'

'Yes.' If I could reach down the receiver, squeeze him around the throat, and extrude his brains through the telephone line like toothpaste into my living room, I would. However, I'm trying to remain calm. 'You still haven't found us.'

Needless to say, just at the point that I've loaded the kids and the luggage into the car, the taxi driver arrives in the road and cruises along at walking speed looking for our house. This shouldn't be all that hard, because there are only six houses in our road, and ours is the only one of them with all the lights on and the front door open at 3 a.m. on a winter morning. I run into the street, beckon him towards the house, consider and dismiss the idea of violence, and transfer cargo and passengers into an Austin Maestro, the back of which evidences the unmistakable aroma of someone, no doubt on their way home from the office party just a few hours ago, having been copiously sick. Excellent; only fifteen miles to go to Heathrow with the children gagging.

I feel fairly sure that when eventually I die of the massive heart attack, it's going to be either in a traffic jam or at an airport. The problem is that, like every Grumpy Old Man, I just hate queuing. As soon as I see the line of people snaking this way and that way between tapes fastened to little stainless steel pillars, I feel the anger welling up inside me. I just can't help it. I've tried, Lord knows I've tried, but I just can't help it.

Literally everything about airports is guaranteed to get on the tits of the Grumpy Old Man. It's one of the situations, like getting involved in the NHS, in which you stop being a person and start being 'processed'. All they want to do is to 'process' you with as little trouble as possible, and therefore everything that happens is entirely for their convenience, and none of it for your own.

Aside from all that, there are far too many people, and they're all decked out in their holiday gear. I don't know what it is, but something about other people in their holiday clothes makes Grumpy Old Men start twitching. Somewhere up ahead of you, standing just to one side of the queue, a bloke and his wife are pretending that they don't quite know how the queue works and are inveigling themselves into it. You can't work out why the people they're inserting themselves in front of don't remonstrate, but they are usually Japanese and look even more confused.

Or maybe someone, somewhere along the line ahead of you, has been holding a place for Doreen and Eddie and their three brats, and so Doreen and Eddie and the brats think it's OK to push past you to get alongside their friends. Or sometimes they might say something like 'Hope you don't mind … our friends saved us a place', and you want to say, 'No of course I don't mind. It's fine that we and our kids got up at 2 a.m. to get here on time, so that you and your kids could stay in bed and send your idiot friends to enable you to jump the queue.' But you don't say that, do you? If you're my wife you smile politely and say, 'No that's fine, you go ahead,' and if you're me you just grunt.

There are women at four check-in desks, but only one of them is operational, because the others are still adjusting their seats or tapping at the keyboard of the computer, or passing the time of day with the swarthy-looking bloke with the ridiculous moustache who may be in charge of the baggage. Doing anything and everything possible to avoid looking up and noticing that there are the best part of 800 people ahead of them, all of whom have spent thousands of pounds on this trip, and all of whom are nevertheless to be treated like so many cattle; a tag on the earlobe and down the shoot on the way to the stun-gun.

The initial excitement of getting up early with the prospect of air travel has worn off long ago, and now the kids are tired and irritable and swinging on your arm saying, 'When are we getting on the plane?', and you're saying, 'Soon kids, be good now,' even though you know there are still many hours to go and many hurdles to cross before boarding.

And you also know that every other plane that is due to board at the same time will board on schedule, and the indicator board will indicate 'wait in lounge' next to your flight right up to five minutes past the time the plane should actually be leaving, and then it'll give an 'expected boarding time' of thirty minutes (at least) after you were originally due to take off.

In the meantime, all you can do is gaze around the soulless, artless shops, personed (one can no longer say 'manned') by people who look as though they've had their personalities removed by micro-surgery, and a facial expression painted on which represents a more perfect mixture of hope and contempt than even the most imaginative actor could invent.

Anyway, as this book isn't about holidays as such, we won't go into all the rest of the stuff about airports, air travel, and generally being processed and fucked about that they involve. Let's move right along to our arrival in Orlando so that we can get onto celebrating my wife's idea of having 'Christmas in the Magic Kingdom'.

You've probably done this yourself; it certainly seems as though half of the bloody world has. We get off the plane and into a sultry, cloudy day, which looks as though it could easily clear up and become sunny. Or could end up in a thunderstorm. We go to the baggage hall and stand alongside the conveyor belt to wait for our luggage.

Being a Grumpy Old Man, and with nothing better to do while waiting, I've spent quite a lot of time trying to work out what you have to do in order to get your bags off the plane first, so you can get into the queue for a hire-car first, and be on your way first. Over the years I've tried arriving first, I've tried arriving last, and I've tried arriving between first and last, and not once have I ever managed to get my bags off the flight first, or anywhere near first, or even together.

On this occasion, miraculously, one of our bags was among the first twenty or so to appear on the conveyor belt, so I grabbed it and eyed the exit, planning a quick getaway. This was the bag containing a load of my wife's clothes and Lizzie's presents. From that moment, approximately forty minutes passed while I examined bags of every shape, size and colour, trying to persuade myself that maybe it was a bit like mine. No second bag. Excellent – no clothes for me, and no Christmas presents for Matt.

Well, you know what happens next; sure I've had my share of occasions when my bags were lost and ended up in Cairo, as has everyone else, but this wasn't one of them. We were just at the point of despair, the luggage hall empty of everyone except a few languid Puerto Rican porters, when the conveyor belt abruptly started moving again and a solitary black suitcase emerged from the depths. Our relief was slightly inching ahead of our irritation by then, so we just grabbed it and made for the exit.

All this was before 9/11, so in those days it's fair to say that US Customs was reasonably relaxed; and since 99 out of every 100 passengers arriving from the UK were Disney-bound, they didn't feel quite as inclined towards invasive body searches as they do these days. Which is just as well. A gloved finger up the arse is bad enough

when you're physically and mentally pre-
pared for it at the prostate clinic; as a start
to a fantasy holiday it leaves a lot to be
desired. Unless of course you are... No no,
probably that's a good place to leave it.

I said previously that this was an unfeasibly inexpensive package, including flights,
hotels and a hire-car, and so we dutifully
trooped into the arrivals hall and started
searching for the Cheepo car-rental desk. I
looked along a line of maybe twenty different companies, Hertz, Avis, American,
Budget, Getuthere, Getuhome, Getustuffed
or whatever. Each of them had bright, smil-
ing and efficient-looking people dressed in
uniforms behind the desks, and no one
standing in front. Only one little plastic-
fronted cubicle cut into the wall had a
queue of fifty people standing in front of it,
and see if you can guess which one that was?

An hour and a half later, which is two and
a half hours after we'd got off the plane, and
ten and a half hours since we'd left London,
and thirteen and a half hours after we'd left
our beds, we're at the front of the queue and
being asked a long series of complex questions about which 'waivers' we want. And it
turns out, as you already know, that the package we've booked entitles us to a car which
Noddy would have trouble fitting into, with
no air-conditioning, and insurance cover
which makes you liable to replace the vehicle

if it is scraped by another car when it's not moving, or for damages of up to $40m if you should accidentally run over a hair which has previously fallen from the head of anyone who knows the cell-phone number of lawyers-4-U, or whatever. Anyway, once you've rectified all that, it turns out that the 'free' car hire will cost at least an extra £25 a day if we don't want to risk arrest and a life of penury in the event of the smallest accident.

Then comes the fun part.

'This here's a map of the Orlando area, showing all the attractions.' One has a sense that the woman has been through this routine once or twice before, and is very keen to get through it now with few or no questions. As she speaks, she is scribbling circles in biro on the map. 'This here is the Magic Kingdom, this here is the Epcot Center, this here is Universal Studios and this here is Seaworld.' Already the map looks like it's been superimposed by the Olympic rings.

'This here is the Wild-West theme show, which is affiliated to Cheepo rent-a-car and where you can get a $15 discount off your ticket if you arrive on a Wednesday between the hours of 4 and 6 p.m. Your coupon is in your information pack. This here is Wet and Wild water attraction which is also affiliated to Cheepo rent-a-car...'

All this continues for about ten minutes, but none of it penetrates our heads because

164

all we want to do at this moment is to be shown to the car and pointed in the direction of our hotel so that we can get into a room, throw ourselves onto a bed and cry ourselves to sleep.

Eventually we are asked to ride on a golf-cart which takes us about a mile and a half to where 50,000 identical cars are parked. I load up our stuff, install the kids into the back, and then sit in the front passenger seat. The kids think this is hilarious, but my wife is alarmed about the effects of jet-lag on my driving, so for the sake of the kids I pretend I knew all along the driver sits on the left in America, and was just having a laugh.

Like most Grumpy Old Men, I pride myself on my sense of direction, and in any case I've got a clear feeling that most of the people arriving at Orlando airport want to go to the same place, so the powers that be are going to have made it as simple as possible to get there. We're staying somewhere called the Disney Radisson Hyatt Regency Hilton or something, which sounds as though it must be pretty central, and so I feel that if for some reason I can't follow the map with all the Olympic rings scribbled on it, I'm fairly certain I'm going to be able to follow signposts.

Well, have you ever done this? If so, you know the rest. Within seconds you are hurtled from the relative calm and safety of

165

the car park into a ten-lane highway in which everyone is behaving as though they're in a scene from *Bullitt*. There are lanes filtering in and lanes filtering out at distances of what seems like about twenty yards apart, and overhead signs which appear to bear absolutely no relation to anything you can see on your map.

Of course you're familiar with all this because you've seen variations of it in so many American movies. Except that usually Sandra Bullock is hanging out of a window of a coach or Steve McQueen is walking along the top of one, ducking under the overhead signs. The only trouble is that usually you've watched this with half an eye as you lean across to pop another cheddar-flavoured Dorito into the sour cream dip, and so you haven't been paying attention to the rules of lane discipline. Neither do you know at what point ahead of the exit marked 'downtown' you are supposed to cut directly across five lanes without indicating.

Now, suddenly, you're a character in the movie yourself, driving along at an alarming speed, and fully expecting the bloke in the car next to you to pull out a revolver and start shooting. Or for whatever is the local version of a 'black and white' (can't say I remember; maybe blue and white?) to loom large in your rear view and start flashing its lights and sounding its siren, and then for

166

some variation of Eddie Murphy to come and start smart-mouthing you.

I once inadvertently ran a red light (I believe that is the local expression) in Texas and was pulled over by a cop straight out of central casting. Chewing tobacco, the whole nine yards. He wasn't at all clear that you could drive in America with a UK licence, but when eventually he came reluctantly to the conclusion that probably I wasn't going to be a candidate for the electric chair, he asked me, 'Do you have red lights in England?' For once thinking quickly, I said, 'Yes we do, but they are the only things I've seen so far that are bigger in the UK than they are in Texas.' That broke the spell and he let me on my way without so much as belabouring me with his night-stick. I guess that must probably be because I'm not a black man.

Anyway, back in Florida, you are still hurtling along, hoping against hope that eventually you'll see something that resembles the name of one of the districts you've been told to look out for. But you don't. You just don't. By now the kids are tired and tetchy, and my wife would also be getting tired and tetchy, except that she can see that I'm also getting very tired and very tetchy, and it doesn't do to allow all those things to happen at the same time. So she goes silent; which makes everything even worse.

'I thought you were paying attention when they gave us the directions,' I say. She remains silent. She and I both know that this is an outrageous and unreasonable suggestion on my part – it's well known and understood that navigation falls into my area of responsibility. But hey, I'm tired and jet-lagged and feeling unreasonable. Wanna make something of it?

We could, of course, fill the whole chapter with the car ride but you'd get bored, and anyway I can't honestly say that I recall how we eventually managed to find our hotel. Let's just say that by the time we arrived at the Disney Radisson Hyatt Regency Hilton (Downtown), we'd already been to the Disney Radisson Hyatt Regency Hilton (Uptown) and via everywhere else in Florida up to and including the Okefenokee swamp. I also remember that the car-hire firm had said it would be fifteen miles and that our trip-meter said thirty-five.

If you've ever been to Disneyland in Florida at Christmas, you know what it's like. And if you haven't – take my advice – don't go. Did the kids all in all have a wonderful time? Of course they did – they were aged seven and nine and scientists have proven that these are the ages of greatest susceptibility to things Disney. It's like the Jesuits; if you can get them at seven, you've got them for life.

Even the most hardened cynic would have to agree that these guys do it well. Boy, do they know their market – but then so they should, because they've been doing it for years. The combination of oversized characters, vast portions of junk food and fizzy drinks, ears with everything, has been proven to be irresistible to small children.

However, before we go any further with either praise or criticism, it is of interest (at least to our publishers, if not to you) to take note that while Disney is all cute and cuddly on the outside, there's a tough and dangerous inside. There's a well-known mantra in the media industry that you 'don't fuck with Mickey'; which is an engaging way of saying that if you do, they'll hunt you down mercilessly, litigate you into a state of a masticated kiwifruit, and then spit out the pips (if kiwifruit have pips).

This being the case, you can see why it might be with some trepidation that I say – just as a sort of aside – that Disney was responsible for the outbreak of the Second World War and all the consequences that flowed from it. (I now have a vivid image of a lot of very smart and slick lawyers reaching for their phones, so I'd better move on before they dial the number and a sequence of events begins which can end only with me being scraped off the bottom of Mickey's oversized shoes.)

It's well known that Adolf Hitler was at one time a housepainter, but it seems – did you know this? – that he was also a very keen animator. Weird, huh? Anyway, I heard that at one time he applied for a job with Walt Disney, as a cartoonist. I know, I know, it's hard to believe, but it's true (allegedly).

Anyway, can you imagine the scene? Presumably it's an interview panel of some sort, like we have now, and a succession of people are coming in, bringing samples of their work and maybe answering some questions. You can see the interviewers flicking through some of the doodlings brought by Herr Hitler. 'Yes, Mr Hitler,' you can well imagine them saying, 'interesting stuff. However, when we said draw your idea of some ideal leisure space, we were thinking more of a playground rather than a map of Poland.'

The point is that he didn't get the job, but can you imagine what would have happened if he had? If they'd just had one more vacancy and had said, maybe over a frankfurter during the coffee break, 'I don't know, why don't we give Mr Hitler a chance? If he doesn't make it as an animator, he did at least have some interesting ideas about crowd control.'

If that had happened, presumably Adolf wouldn't have gone off and formed the Nazi Party, wouldn't have become Chancellor of all-Germany, wouldn't have invaded Poland, wouldn't have started the Second World War, and the whole course of twentieth-century history would have been entirely different. All because of a botched-up interview at Disney.

We're all used to the idea of the law of unintended consequence. Or all that stuff about a butterfly farting in the Amazon and a tidal wave in Tokyo or whatever, but I think this one takes the biscuit. If you'd been able to tell the blokes on the interview panel who went home that evening and told the missus a little anecdote about the funny little chap with the toothbrush moustache you met today, that their decision would lead to the deaths of 20 million people, they would probably be entitled to be a bit bemused.

Maybe it's something that Simon Cowell might usefully keep in mind when he's being rude to all those little wankers on *The X Factor*. One of them may go off and form a political party... Anyway, fascinating though all that is, I'm not at all sure how it got into a book about Christmas. However, it did, so let's let it go and resume our trip to Florida.

Florida at Christmas, as anyone who has ever been can testify, is the world's greatest queuing experience. It's a commonplace that, in contrast to our European neighbours, most British people don't seem to mind queuing. In my mind that simply means that usually they don't start rioting.

But as we heard at the airport, Grumpy Old Men simply hate it. Of course, we have to put up with it in our cars, to get on buses, etc., but ordinarily we will go a very long way out of our way to avoid being in a queue.

So to find yourself paying thousands of pounds to go on holiday, only then to stand in a series of queues of a length you associate with trying to buy a loaf of bread in communist Russia, comes a bit hard. Add to that the fact that your kids are very young, inclined to tire easily and become troublesome if hanging about in one place for too long, and you have the perfect holiday cocktail.

All this would have been bad enough, but in our case it was exacerbated by something which I've promised not to pass on to you, but as Matt (now aged eighteen, then seven) has irritated me recently almost beyond endurance, I'm going to. And that is that quite frequently, we'd wait for about an hour and a half to get to the front of the queue, only for him to bottle it and decide that he didn't want to go on the ride after all. Can you imagine?

Foremost in my memory among a number of examples, was the *Jaws* ride – which I think is probably at Universal Studios. In the year we went it was brand new, state of the art, and everybody was talking about it. The queue, needless to say, went back for bloody miles. Sure, it has to be admitted that if people are going to have to queue, these guys organise it well. It's not going to be a very long stretch-out thin line, which has the effect of merely emphasising that it's nothing more nor less than a lot of people waiting. No, these people organise it in the form of a snake, the various coils divided up with barriers, so that you can't really tell if the people standing next to you are queuing in front of you or queuing behind you. And you can't really tell how long the queue is, or how long it will take to get to the front of it. In fact, you can't really tell anything, except that, once again, you are being 'processed'.

Every ten yards or so there is a screen showing promotions for the ride. These are supposed to have the effect of heightening the anticipation and presumably making the apparently endless wait feel worthwhile. What they also did, in our case, was heighten the terror being felt by Matt. So that as more and more time passed, instead of getting more and more excited, he was getting more and more petrified.

To come to the point, we had been waiting in that queue for exactly an hour and forty-five minutes, we seemed to be within screaming distance of the front, when Matt's nerve finally cracked under the strain and he froze, rooted to the spot.

'What's the matter, Matt?' Lizzie had been

the first to notice.

'I don't want to go on it.'

'What?' said the rest of us, each taking one part in a three-part harmony.

'I don't want to go on it.'

And he didn't. Which meant that either my wife or I couldn't go on it either because we couldn't leave Matt standing there on his own. And we didn't have long to decide.

There followed a brief moment of torment, during which my brain was working at 100 miles per hour. I want to go on the ride, but I know that if I do, I'll feel guilty about it for the rest of the holiday. On the other hand, if I don't, while I'll be pissed off at having queued all this time and then missed the thing I've been waiting for, I'll have accumulated quite a lot of martyr points – which might stand me in good stead at some other time in the holiday.

I make a quick decision. My wife must go on the ride with Lizzie. Matt and I will go to the end and wait.

We do, and it being Christmas, I indulge Matt by doing and saying whatever I can to make him feel better about being a bloody big cissy. I resist pointing out the hundreds of kids younger and smaller than him who are coming off the ride, soaked to the skin but absolutely exhilarated. I talk about another ride which looked to be every bit as much fun but isn't so scary. I am the very model of an understanding and indulgent father – leaving it only until now – when he is eighteen and stroppy – to expose his humiliation to the wider world.

So everything is big in America, and Christmas in America is no exception. It's big parades with big cartoon characters with big shoes and big ears. It's big drinks and big burgers with very, very big orders of fries on the side. It's big people, with very, very big arses, usually silhouetted in tight jeans. It's big firework displays, big lights and Christmas trees that are big enough to be seen from outer space.

The trouble is that, in Florida at least, it's also hot. And the mix of a very sweaty Santa and fake snow seems somehow just too American. For those of us who grew up amid the festive slush of the big-city suburbs, hot and Christmas don't readily mix. We want cold and damp, so that in theory at least we can rush out for long cheery walks to bring a rosy glow to our cheeks, and then come back and warm ourselves in front of the open log fire, with the smell of pine needles permeating the air. Well, at least back in the UK that could happen. I suppose.

So is 'getting away from it all' a solution to the persecution that Christmas represents for the Grumpy Old Man? Well, I'd like to give an honest answer, but then, you don't fuck with Mickey.

12

Feeding the 5,000

One thing about Grumpy Old Men that might surprise you (unless you are one) is that we don't get on very well with guilt.

What do I mean?

Well, put it this way. There's a whole lot of jobs that Grumpy Old Men want to have done, but the trouble is that we don't want to do them ourselves. So, as we want them done but don't want to do them, the chances are that they're likely to end up being done by somebody else. Someone like the wife.

Which you'd think would fall into the category of what Grumpy Old Men might call 'a result', but unfortunately it's not quite as simple as that. Because then we feel guilty, and we don't like feeling guilty. Sometimes we want to relax, but it's only possible to truly relax when you're feeling free of guilt.

So, if you want to give a Christmas present to a Grumpy Old Man that he'll really appreciate, do something for him that you know he wants done, but doesn't want to do himself. Sounds simple enough, but here's the tricky bit – you need to find a way to make it look like a pleasure for you to do it, so that he doesn't feel guilty about it.

Geddit?

There are a lot of aspects of Christmas that fall into this category. For example, Grumpy Old Men certainly don't want to have to go shopping for presents but, though we do rather a good job of feigning indifference, we'd probably be uncomfortable if nobody did it at all.

Another one is cards. I always say that I don't care if we send Christmas cards or not, but I guess that if my wife didn't set to and take on the task, at some point I might feel as though at least a few cards should have been sent.

Also, I always complain about all the stuff relating to the Christmas tree but if nobody else took care of it... No, come to think of it, that's the exception. If no one in our household bothered with a Christmas tree, that would be fine with me.

However, probably because over the years I've made myself so objectionable when asked to participate in things like this – present-buying, card-sending, tree-erecting – my wife has decided that it is easier to just get on and do them herself. Which would be fine, except that then the trouble is that I sometimes feel guilty. And secretly I think that if she really loved me, she would not only do all these things quietly and very

177

effectively, as she does now. She'd also find a way of doing them without making me feel guilty that I'm not helping.

I have a feeling that I may be losing the sympathy of the women voters here, but hey, what's the point if you can't be honest?

You know what they say about stopping digging, but we've come this far, so what the hell? The worst of these things – the very worst thing that we absolutely don't want to do at Christmas, but we know needs to be done – is the Christmas food shopping.

It seems beyond dispute, for some reason, that we need an enormous amount of food to tide us over the two days before the shops open again. We appear to want, on these few days at least, to be able to forget about our diets and eat a whole selection of unwise confections in implausible combinations with exotic savouries. We seem compelled to eat far more than we ever would in any circumstances in the rest of the year, up to and way beyond the point of discomfort and even pain. We seem in danger of becoming the victim of an anxiety attack if we have less than five times the amount of food that could possibly be eaten by a reasonable group of people in the time available to them – rather as though we were expecting the equivalent of the siege of Stalingrad to begin at any moment.

Anyone careless enough not to have

hoarded away several months' supply of crisps, Doritos, sour cream and chive dip, guacamole, sausage rolls, cheese straws and thin chocolate mints will be the first to have to run desperately out into the icy wastes and throw themselves on the mercy of the marauding armies.

OK, OK, I know we're getting a bit carried away here, but the point is that we seem to need to do a lot of shopping for food in the run-up to Christmas.

Just before we proceed to what I think readers may find a surprising turn of events, I should explain that I have not always been a Grumpy Old Man. Yes, of course I've always been grumpy, and yes, of course I've been a man since I was a boy. But contrary to the fixed views of my children, I haven't always been old. And once, just once, when I was just two of the three elements which make up our present condition, I actually did the main food shopping at Christmas.

I know, I know – you find that weird, and looking back on it, I find it weird too. I can't remember the actual circumstances, but I think that maybe the kids were sick, one set of the in-laws was arriving early, my wife had the flu; anyway it was some combination of stuff that, when mixed together, brought about a wholly unexpected reaction in me.

'I'll do the food shopping tomorrow.'

No response.

'Did you hear what I said? I said that I'd do the food shopping tomorrow.'

Still no response. I wondered for a moment if the virus had caused my wife some temporary deafness – and I'll leave you to put in the Pinter-esque pauses in what follows.

'Hello?'

'What?'

'Did you hear what I said?'

'Yes.'

'Then why aren't you answering?'

'Because you're not.'

'Not what?'

'Not doing the food shopping tomorrow.'

'Yes, I am.'

'No, you're not.'

'Why not?'

'Because you can't do it.'

'Why not?'

'Because you don't know how to do it.'

So now, having no doubt been rather full of self-sacrifice and nobility in making my offer, I'm beginning to feel a bit indignant.

'Well, silly me. I thought it was a question of taking that piece of paper on the sideboard with 300 items written on it, getting in the car, going to the supermarket, filling the trolley with all the items, paying for them, and coming home.'

'Yes, it is. And that's why you can't do it.'

I won't go on to report the whole debate in

180

direct speech because *tempus fugit*, but what it came down to was that I wasn't to be trusted to choose the right kind of pineapple, the right degree of ripeness of the melons, the right variety of stuffing, the right make of olives, the right type of horse for the chestnuts... Well, you get the idea.

So in the end the agreement was reached that we'd get up early the following morning to try to beat the crowds, and that I would go along to help. Dawn came early next day (actually it came at about the same time as usual, but it's one of those expressions you often find in unfolding narratives, so I thought I'd throw it in). Dawn came early next day and my wife's flu had worsened. In fact, it was so bad that she, against all her instincts and wishes, had to concede that there was no choice but for me to go food shopping on my own.

She told me to get the list from the kitchen, and as I returned up the stairs I felt like one of those obnoxious dogs from the TV advertisements walking along with a toilet roll trailing along behind me. From a quick glance, it seemed straightforward enough to me; three and a half hundredweight of King Edwards, two and a half pecks of broccoli, half an orchard of 'nice apples' – not horrible apples you understand, it seems we wanted nice ones.

Anyway I had to hand over the list and

then to tune into, and commit to memory, the narrative accompaniment. Occasionally during this process I was required to repeat something back verbatim as evidence that I had properly absorbed it.

'Try to get those very nice oranges like the ones I got three weeks ago and which Matt liked so much; sometimes they're tucked away behind the tangerines. Get satsumas rather than mandarins because the last lot we had were a bit dry. Don't get the tomatoes already in the plastic bags because some of them can be a bit soft; you need to pick up each one carefully and you'll see a bag on the side where you can weigh your own. Get just two pounds if they're not very nice but get two kilos if they're nice and firm, and in that case try to make sure some of them are a bit green.'

I started out in reasonable good faith trying to remember all this, but all the time I had half an eye on the clock and a vivid mental image of the car park filling up, and the walk from the car to the store with the wobbly trolley getting longer and longer. All I wanted to do was to get on my way.

Eventually, with about the same level of briefing as the crew of Apollo 13 going round in my head, I get to the car. It's 8 a.m. I should be in good time to beat the rush.

Well, have you ever been in Newcastle, or any other great footballing city, on the day

of the first match of the football season? As
you get nearer and nearer to the ground,
you become more and more aware that
every living being anywhere around you is
heading in the same direction, and as you
begin to get close to your destination, it
seems that the whole of humanity is con-
verging with an uncompromising determination on one place.

The queue of traffic to get into the slip
road – which is itself about a half a mile
from the car park – was backed up another
half a mile onto the dual carriageway. A
glance towards the car park itself reminded
me of those scenes in *Troy – The Movie*
where they're preparing for the impending
conflict. Vast armies of people, their loins
girded for battle, and ready for the attack.

An hour and a half later I managed to park
about a quarter of a mile from the store
entrance, having twice been gazumped by
those Smart cars which are more or less a
shopping trolley with a motor, and finally
gazumping an old lady driving a Morris
1000 which looked as though it had been
inherited from her father. I then wrestled an
old man to the ground in a fight for the last
trolley, and emerged triumphant into the
supermarket. I looked around, my eyes
blinking in genuine amazement.

What was it like? What on earth was it like?
Words fail me to adequately describe it, but

here goes.

Firstly, it was vast. Think Terminal 1 at Heathrow and add 50 per cent of the space again. I mean huge. Acres and acres of shelves stretching far into the distance. I mean *really* huge.

Secondly, it was packed. Think Wembley on Cup Final day and increase the density by a factor of 20 per cent. Think Oxford Street on a Saturday, or Trafalgar Square on New Year's Eve. Think the Northern Line. Think packed.

Thirdly, it was bedlam. Think – well, just think about 3,000 people in a confined space with sharp corners and nothing to absorb the noise, and all of them shouting at each other versions of 'Do you want satsumas or mandarins? Eh? What did you say? I can't hear you above this fucking racket.' Then overlay that with a level of piped music of the kind you're going to be hearing in the old folks' home on the day the lights finally go out. I swear that if they'd been playing 'I Wish It Could Be Christmas Every Day' at this point, I'd have phoned for an ambulance as a precaution against my imminent collapse.

And all this under a grid of fluorescent lights which last had a use in the interrogation room at Nuremberg.

I stood there gazing at it, jaw wide open, and I just wanted to scream. And scream.

And scream. However, I didn't; and if I had, no one would have heard me or otherwise taken any notice. Indeed, quite a few other people around me seemed to be doing more or less that.

No, I fished around in my pocket for the list, located it, and then found to my surprise that the long sheet of paper seemed to be about half the length I remembered. I looked at the bottom of the list, only to find it torn off halfway through the word 'celery', and searched in my pockets for the rest of it. There was no sign. I tried to summon up a mental picture of how long the list had originally been, and therefore how much of it was missing, and managed to convince myself that I had all but an inch or two. Nothing for it but to press on.

So – does anyone on the planet understand the science of where anything goes in a supermarket? Does anyone?

Sure, we all know that they like to put the fruit and vegetables near the door so you'll get an impression of fresh produce as you walk in. Maybe you'll think you've stumbled into a farm or something. We all know that they like to bake bread somewhere near the back so the smell will permeate your nostrils and make you hungry and therefore want to buy more stuff. So we can follow our noses to the bread. We all know that they're going to put the sweets and chocolates next to the till in the hope that you will find them irresistible as you wait your turn, and that if you don't your kids will.

But where the fuck do they put the cornflour? Is that under baking? Or cereals? Or somewhere near the gravy mix? Is it somewhere near the corn oil, and if so, is the corn oil somewhere near everything else in bottles, or near the lard which is itself somewhere near the margarine?

Why do you suppose it is that there is a selection of boxes of bloody awful chocolates at the end of every second aisle, but the main area where they'll have the particular brand of those little-mints-whose-name-we-can't-remember-but-which-come-in-a-perspex-box-and-are-individually-wrapped-in-pale-green-foil is nowhere to be found?

And why, just as you think you may be gaining momentum, are there three aisles full of nothing else but varieties of dog food?

Mercifully the distance of time and space since this trauma has blurred some of the details, but looking back on it, I would imagine that an efficient shopper might have had to walk maybe a mile and a half to collect everything on the top two-thirds of our list. I reckon I must have walked at least three. No kidding. Three miles at least, and that was just to fill the first trolley. When that was full I recklessly double-parked it in the middle of an aisle, grabbed another one from a blind man, and started filling it. When I returned with my second full trolley three quarters of an hour later to collect the first one, it was causing a tailback along the thoroughfare halfway from the Cheerios to West Ham.

With two trolleys full, and more or less at the end of my list with the exception of a couple of items I couldn't decipher or had given up trying to find, I tried to envisage what could have been written on the bottom part of the list which was missing.

What had my wife said from her sick-bed? I thought that it might be something about cream, but I knew it wasn't anything quite as simple as 'cream', so perhaps it was something that sounded like 'freme fraire' or some sort of cream substitute. After another fifteen minutes of searching, during which the back of my ankles was twice dunched by an out-of-control trolley wielded by a Coked-up seven-year-old boy on behalf of his delinquent mother, I located the fridge where the cream was and scanned the rows of tubs for something which might jog my memory.

Sour cream? No. Double cream? No. Single cream? No. Half-cream? No. Whipping cream? No. At this point I sensed a quick gear-change going on. Yogurt? No. Mousse? No. Fools? No. And now I think I must have come too far so I start scanning in the other direction. Petits filous? No. Sundaes? No. Cottage cheese? Must have come too far. Look up, and there's a row of the equivalent of all the above but made from soya instead of milk. Look down, and there's another row of the above except low-fat, half-fat, full fat or extremely fat. Can I find anything resembling or sounding like 'freme fraire'? Can I hell. I take about half a gallon of double cream and put it in the trolley, which is by now groaning under the weight.

What else? Well, honestly I couldn't really remember then, so I sure as hell can't remember now, but suffice it to say that I reached the conclusion that we'd survive without whatever it was. Hell, Mao Tse Tung's Red Army could have survived Christmas on what I'd already bought.

So – off to the check-out. That's always a lot of fun, isn't it? Queuing of any kind, as I've discussed elsewhere, always brings out the best in Grumpy Old Men. Merely the sight of all those thousands of people arranging themselves into their rows as instructed, makes me start to hyperventilate. Wide aisles, thin aisles, one basket, five items or less, self-service and customer service which may or may not also be a check-out. If you don't queue at it, it is; and if you do queue at it, it isn't.

There is so much about this that feels oppressive for a Grumpy Old Man that he can easily begin to take it personally. Which is when he can start to become a bloody nuisance. Rory McGrath entertained us with his saga over 'five items or less' which, as he pointed out, should really be 'five items or fewer'. Indeed, he not only pointed it out to us, but he also pointed it out to the store manager, and was delighted to notice a week later that it had been changed to 'five items or fewer'. However, being a proper Grumpy, Rory had only just got going.

Now he'd stand in the 'five items or fewer' queue and look around him at the contents of other people's baskets. If a person had a bag with six oranges in it, was that one item with six items in it, or six items? 'If it was me it was one item, if it was someone else it was six items. Out of the queue.' Needless to say, Rory has been banned from quite a few supermarkets.

Rick Wakeman's pet hate is the woman with the daughter. She's standing in the queue, having her items go through the check-out, but all the while sending her daughter back and forth into the maelstrom to collect the stuff she's forgotten. 'Oh,' she'll yell halfway across the store, 'and don't forget to get a large carton of tampons.' Or the old lady with the coupons. 'Half a penny off this. Tuppence halfpenny off that.' Rick says he'd rather pay her entire bloody food bill than wait any longer, and sometimes has.

My personal nightmare is the idea that the queue you are standing in is always moving more slowly than the one next to you. No matter how hard I try, I simply can't stop myself from constantly checking where I would be if I had joined the queue next to me, and whether I would have arrived at the counter faster in that queue than this. Though I've tried to make something of a science out of choosing the right queue over the years, I reckon that I still get it wrong five times out of six; usually because the person just ahead of me will have mislaid their purse, or their wallet, or their cheque book, or their loyalty card or something, and meanwhile I'm in imminent danger of losing my fucking mind.

And what is it about those little dividers that separate one person's shopping from the next? How much aggro have they caused over the years? You can be in danger of reaching for them too soon, reaching for them too late, or even placing them at an angle where there may be some ambiguity about what lies which side of it. The division of Jerusalem has hardly caused more friction.

Eventually it's your turn and you have to ceremonially take every item you've taken off the shelves and put into your trolley, out of your trolley and stack them carefully on the counter, making sure that the meringue nests don't get crushed under the two hundredweight of King Edwards, and the prawn and lettuce sandwich you bought for the journey home gets packed within easy reach at the top of a carrier bag.

Usually there is no one to help you to pack, and so you have to locate a bundle of plastic bags, and then – can you get the opening to peel apart? Can anyone? I'm pushing here and rubbing there and wetting my fingers and trying to prise open what turns out to be a seam. Exactly how hard can it be to manufacture plastic bags so that you can find and open the hole where the items are supposed to go in? How hard can that be? But does anybody give a stuff? Of course they bloody well don't. So it's just another thing to drive us crazy.

Having put all this stuff into the trolley, and then taken it out of the trolley, the items you've bought are now going back into the trolley for the ride to the car. The queue of people waiting to get out into the car park looks like those rows of dejected refugees you've seen in the newsreels with all their worldly goods piled up on a wheelbarrow in front of them. You've got two, both with the inevitable dodgy wheel, and so manoeuvring back to the car makes you feel like a runner-up in *It's a Knockout*. (Remember that?)

Eventually you locate the car, which you've stupidly parked facing outwards so you can't get behind it with the trolley to load the boot. And since you parked, some numb-nuts has parked his huge and filthy 4 x 4 about four inches away from the side of your car, and on the other side there is a large white van. So now there's not enough room to push the trolleys through the gap, you resolve to put them somewhere out of harm's way while you get into the car, drive it out, do a three-point turn in a confined space and drive forwards into the gap – all the while being careful not to run into a careless pedestrian or, worse still, your shopping trolleys.

The only way you can get into the car is to squeeze through the gap, efficiently trans-ferring four months' worth of mud from his wing-mirror to your jacket. Then you notice that the zip on your jacket has left a long scratch along the side of his vehicle, which leaves you hoping that he's not going to return before you've driven away.

On this occasion I eventually opened the driver's door, only to see the bottom third of the original shopping list fall out of the door jamb and onto the tarmac. I picked it up. Oh shit. There were at least ten items on it, including more wrapping paper, sweet pickled onions and a box of Black Magic, just in case Linda's mum should happen to pop in when she's visiting her daughter next door – or something.

So now I'm in a dilemma. Is there any way

I can face going back into the Mines of Mordor to get this bloody stuff? I think that maybe the clue to the answer lies in the tone of the question. No way, Jose. I'm out of here. Or at least I would be if it were not for the queue of cars stretching as far as the eye can see, and clogging up all the access roads in every direction.

It appears that the whole of humanity wants to get into and out of this particular supermarket on this particular day and, to make matters worse, the vast majority want to fill up with slightly discounted petrol on their way out. So the queue to rejoin the highway is further backed up because one of the exit lanes has twenty cars on it waiting to turn onto the forecourt.

When and why did supermarkets start selling petrol? You'd think there would be some limit to their insatiable greed to sell you everything anyone could possibly want. But presumably it was that decision which led the garages to start to sell groceries. So that now when all you want to do is part with £50 as quickly as possible for your tank of unleaded, you're stuck in a queue behind someone buying three tons of washing powder, half a dozen toilet rolls and a range of confectionery stuffed with enough artificial colours and e-numbers to give hallucinations to an ox.

Anyway, to get back to our odyssey. Around

about three hours after I left home, I returned with what I swear was at least fifteen carrier bags full of food. By this time my wife was up and feeling 'a little bit more human' – which was a relief all round because I was feeling distinctly a little more bestial.

She started unpacking my purchases and, to be fair to her, she was doing quite well with comments like: 'Oh good, you got the instant Nescafé for Marjorie – she says she can't drink anything else.' And, 'Those look like nice turnips.' However, as more and more of the items were revealed, I sensed that there were more and more of them which were nearly, but not quite what she would have bought herself. Do you know what I mean? Right size but wrong brand. Wrong size, right brand but wrong variety. Wrong size, wrong brand and wrong variety.

I reckon there were a good five to ten minutes of 'OK, it's not exactly what I asked you to get, but it's fine, we'll make do'. Then there was a period of another five minutes or so of silent unpacking. Then eventually the silence was broken with a big sigh followed by 'I'll have to pop out'. And that was before she realised that I hadn't brought back the Black Magic.

13

In Excelsis Deo

When I left school, I worked for a summer in the library in Lewisham. A not particularly fascinating fact in itself, and the only reason I mention it is that, standing behind the counter in that musty, dusty old library, I frequently used to have to ask people their date of birth.

I didn't like to have to ask, because I always thought it was rather a personal question. However, the point is that I remember hearing people answering by saying '1919' or '1926' and looking up at them and thinking, 'Good God, and this old codger is still breathing!' It was 1969, I was eighteen, and for someone to have been born not that long after the First World War, or in the year of the General Strike and still be upright seemed to me to be remarkable.

I'm fairly certain that I didn't then treat them with anything other than a reasonable amount of indifference because being middle-aged or older, they were completely irrelevant to my life; and at that time, obviously, everything important about life

195

revolved around me.

Nowadays, of course, we're asked our date of birth all the time. Anyone who thinks they need to identify you thinks it's OK to ask, 'Can you just confirm your date of birth, please?' This includes banks, your internet provider, the phone company. Only yesterday I received a call out of the blue from O_2 or whatever they're called, imploring me to renew my contract for another year. Actually, I pointed out, I hadn't been thinking of ending my contract until they made that call; now I was actively contemplating it. This threw the idiot of a kid into a tizzy, but when he regained his composure he asked me if I could confirm my identity by giving him my post code and my date of birth.

'Look, pal,' I said to him, 'I haven't made this call. I don't want anything from you. You've called me and interrupted something very important that I am doing' (trying to think of 6 down in the *Telegraph* crossword). 'Why should I tell you my date of birth?'

So he asked me, 'If I give it to you, will you confirm it?' By now all I want to do is get this little sod off the phone and ordinarily I would just hang up. However, in this case I know that this is what I have learned to call my 'network provider' and as my network provider they are perfectly capable of imposing rather effective sanctions on me, like cutting off my service at the most inconvenient moment, or sending me messages I don't understand about something going on with my 'SIM card'. So I said OK, and he did, and I did, and then went on to whatever bollocks it was we went on to.

Anyway, let's see if we can eventually stagger towards the point I'm trying to make. One of the many enormous irritations about getting older and into your Grumpy Old Man years is that you can sense young people reacting to you with exactly the attitude I displayed towards older people when I was an eighteen-year-old. When I confirmed my date of birth for this little bastard who had called me up, I could hear exactly the same tone in his voice that characterised mine all those years ago when I worked in the library.

When anyone under the age of twenty-five asks the 'D.O.B.' question and gets the answer '1951' they must be thinking, 'Jesus Christ. That's halfway through the last century, and this old fart still thinks he's as entitled to inhale the same air as the rest of us.' They look at you as though you are a character straight out of the history books, which, of course, you are. Or you would be if you'd done anything worth recording.

And that makes us grumpy. We're Grumpy Old Men who generally don't mind admitting that we're getting a bit older, but by and large aren't happy to be treated as though we're geriatrics by little tossers who know nothing and have stewed prunes where their brains should be. So...

Nineteen fifty-one. (I can't write this date in numbers because if I do, my software thinks it's a paragraph heading and wants to indent the type. However, it will kindly let me write it in numbers now that we're in the middle of a paragraph.) 1951. It sounds such a long time ago, doesn't it? And it is, because so much has changed in that time. The world we live in is almost unrecognisable from the one in which we grew up.

You hear it all the time. 'The rate of change is speeding up.' Or marginally more profoundly, 'There's been more change in our lifetime than in any other generation that's ever lived.' Whether or not that's true is probably too big a question to answer here – I guess that people who lived through the start of the Industrial Revolution, or our grandparents whose lifespans saw everything from mankind's first flight to the moon-landing must have a claim.

However, in our short lifetimes we've gone from post-war rationing to 50 per cent of people being overweight or obese. From black and white to HDTV. From pens with nibs to Microsoft XL. From Liberace on a single TV channel to *The Farm* on one of 300. From snakes and ladders to 'Terror Death Force 3' or whatever vile video-game horrible youths are using to practise their violence before going out and performing it. From wind-up gramophones to video iPods. From a walk down to the library to order a book which will come in a fortnight to Google that steers you to 2 million websites in 0.26 seconds if you type in the word 'horseradish'.

We've gone from being able to go about our daily business relatively unmolested to being photographed or taped by Big Brother an average of 300 times a day. We've gone from generally being able to mind our own business to having our supermarket keep a record of how much tinned soup we buy. We've gone from twenty Capstan full-strength every day being good for your throat, to a ban on smoking in all confined public places. And we've gone from being able to ride a motorbike with our hair blowing in the wind to being forced to wear a seatbelt even in the back of the car.

And all that's before we get started. A whole hell of a lot of change for one generation to deal with.

So what has all this got to do with Christmas? Not much, directly, except that I started thinking this morning about the question of who knocks on your front door, and how much about that has changed in the last forty years or so. Which got me thinking about all the rest of it.

When I was a kid, we lived in a flat on a council estate, and people were always knocking on the door. If it wasn't the rent man to collect the weekly rent, it was the electricity man to empty the meter. If it wasn't the milkman to be paid ten bob or so for our two pints of silver-top and one of gold-top per day, it was the insurance man to collect our weekly premiums. If it wasn't the Rington's tea man, it was the rag-and-bone man to see if we had any old clothes we wanted to get rid of (we never did). If it wasn't the bloke who used to sharpen the knives on a grinding-stone mounted in a child's pram, it was the man collecting payments on your catalogue.

Sometimes, I seem to recall, it was a bloke trying to sell you brushes or a miracle new duster, and other times it was the Jehovah's witnesses trying to sell you a miracle new life. Anyway, the point is, someone was always knocking on the door and we were always opening it and having a conversation with them.

What do you do in your household nowadays when someone comes to your front door unexpectedly? It's about 6 p.m., maybe you've just got home from work, and the doorbell rings.

In our household we all look at each other to see if any of us has asked someone to visit and is therefore responsible for this outrage.

Having confirmed that this is not the case, one of us will say, 'I'm not answering that,' and we all agree and get on with our business, waiting for the caller to go away.

Maybe they'll ring the bell once or even twice more, but usually that'll be it.

It's 2006 and we don't want people coming to the house when we're not expecting them. Actually, I don't really want people coming to the house when we *are* expecting them, but that's by the by. We certainly don't want casual callers, and so we've got a notice on our door that gives a short list of strictures to anyone stupid enough to think about ringing the bell.

It says something like: 'No unsolicited mail. No circulars. We never buy anything at the door. You will be expected to produce identification that can be verified. You will be expected to wait in the pouring rain while your identification is verified.' Actually I think it says everything short of 'Fuck off and die', but still occasionally some people are stupid enough to knock and ask if we want the drive resurfaced or our car cleaned.

By now you can probably see where this is going.

Every year, three or four times within a few days, we get a visit from carol singers. And leaving aside the bloody irritation that causes, this is yet another thing that has changed beyond all recognition since

Grumpy Old Men were kids.

When my brother and I were little and living in a block of flats, having a visit from carol singers was all part of the magic of Christmas. Partly it was because it meant that Christmas was coming, which was very exciting; and partly it was because a van would draw up in the street outside, a dozen or so members of the Salvation Army brass band would strike up with their unmistakable, evocative sound, and a choir would start singing in a heavenly chorus. 'Hark the Herald Angels Sing', 'Oh Little Town of Bethlehem', 'We Three Kings of Orient Are'.

It was melodious, it felt festive, it went on for a while; and the best thing about it was that you had plenty of warning, so you could turn off the lights and pretend not to be at home before someone knocked on the door asking for money.

(Actually, this is another of those moments when I can feel my mum looking over my shoulder from her place in heaven and saying, 'Don't write that you little bugger; you know it's not true, and what will people think?' She was the last person in our family, bless her, who gave a stuff about 'what will people think?')

But the point is, it was lovely. They would park on the pavement in front of the flats for about twenty minutes while their helpers went round collecting money from all the flats. They'd play and sing half a dozen carols. There would be a gentle flurry of snow, and if you screwed up your eyes and looked heaven-wards, you could almost imagine Santa doing some practice loops over the rooftops with his sleigh. It made our night, and was well worth six old pennies of anyone's money.

So what is it like now?

There's a knock on the door. We didn't expect it. We all look at each other accusingly. Has anyone invited someone round and not said? Who on earth could this be at this time of night? It's 7.30 for heaven's sake. We're in the middle of dinner. No way we're answering the door; sod them.

The doorbell rings again. We ignore it. In a minute they'll assume we're out and give up. However, the car is outside and the hall lights are on. The doorbell rings again.

Eventually, being undoubtedly the least unpleasant member of our family, my wife usually weakens. We have some glass in the front door, and as soon as they see her in the hallway, it starts.

'Si-i-lent night, ho-o-ly night.'

Aware that this will immediately put me in a bad temper, my wife wants to open the door quickly and complete the transactions. No sooner does she do so than the singing stops. Four little buggers are standing there, probably about fourteen years old, with snot or UHU spread across their filtrums like they've come straight from the glue-sniffers, with their hands stretched out.

'Merry Christmas.'

Sometimes they'll vary the technique and bring with them one of their little brothers or sisters, who'll stand there shivering and looking pathetic in a bobble-hat. The idea is that even the most miserable bastard is less likely to tell a tiny kid where to insert his Christmas carols. Being a bit of a soft touch, my wife doesn't actually want to close the door in their faces while she goes to find her purse. So she leaves it half-open, thereby giving plenty of opportunity for the heating that's been slowly building up in the house all day to be replaced by the icy blast from outside. It also provides plenty of opportunity for the fourteen-year-olds to have a good look at the locks on the door and to make a fast assessment of what there is to steal when they break in a bit later this week.

In the old days the carol singers from the church would be sufficiently discreet to hold out a bag made of cloth, so that your contribution would feel and sound generous even if in reality it was a handful of halfpennies. And once intermingled with the pre-existing donations, no one would ever know. Nowadays, of course, you pass over a pound coin or whatever, and it's taken into a sweaty hand with HATE tattooed across the knuckles and so your generosity or lack of it is immediately evident.

Actually, all this just feels like a not-very-subtle form of extortion; you've got a strong suspicion that if you tell them to get lost, which is what I'd like to do, when you go out in the morning your tyres will be in ribbons. So I'm always trying to work out what is the minimum price of just being left in peace. Fifty pence. Almost certainly not. A pound? Probably, but not definitely. Two pounds then? OK, goddamit, £2 but I'd rather sit up at the window all night with a pellet-gun than pay any more than that.

Now can we get on with dinner and be left the hell alone?

14

'Twas the Night Before Christmas

What is the term you use in your house which means searching cupboards and hiding places high and low to get an illicit glimpse of what you might be receiving by way of presents for Christmas? Do you have a word for it, or is that just us?

We call it 'rootling'. Yes we do, and in the few weeks before Christmas we have a standard saying when we're going out and one person is staying in the house on their own: 'No rootling.'

'As if...' is usually the reply. As if any of us would be so inquisitive and mean-spirited as to want to spoil any surprises on Christmas morning by having a quick rootle ahead of the event. As if.

Did you ever do that? I think the only reason that I have ever subjected our children to that unworthy suspicion is that as kids we absolutely did it ourselves. A bit of rootling. To be honest, that's about as daring as we got. A quick reconnoitre around the airing cupboard, or that big deep shelf at the top of my parents' wardrobe which you had to stand on a chair to be able to reach – and even then you couldn't get your arm right to the back of it.

What a thrill. Occasionally your extended fingers might just touch what felt like a brown paper bag. Press a bit more and you could feel a sharp edge. Could it be the battery-operated machine gun you so desperately wanted? Or the Meccano set we'd willingly die for?

To be honest, I don't think we ever did manage to discover something and thereby spoil the Christmas morning surprise. Probably all we did was to heighten the anticipation, which was already going through the roof.

Anyway, for that reason 'no rootling' has remained a catchphrase in our household, and no rootling has been the golden rule. Which is just as well, because when you think of the enormous amount of bloody trouble you go to on the night before Christmas to make the morning magical, it sure as hell needs to be worth it.

As the kids were growing up, I usually had to work hard right up to Christmas Eve, so that by the time the holiday break came round I was totally and utterly knackered. I've always been of the grumpy persuasion, but I was younger then and this was way before it had been identified as a clinical syndrome as it has now. Anyhow, like every other apprentice Grumpy I know, I just wanted to slump into a chair and watch mindless rubbish on the telly, and then go to bed early. However, my wife always had plans for an elaborate charade which was carefully and cunningly designed to simulate evidence of Santa's visit.

First of all, before the children went to bed, we'd have a little ceremony of leaving stuff on the hearth. A mince pie for Santa and a carrot for Rudolph. Carefully positioned just next to the chimney, so that they are sure to be spotted as soon as our visitors arrive.

'Technically, I don't think Rudolph actually comes down the chimney.'

My wife is unperturbed, and she certainly doesn't want my pedantry to undermine the kids' belief that Rudolph is going to eat the carrot. 'Well, Santa will spot the carrot and take it back up the chimney for him.'

In the drama documentary of this scene, there follows a brief silence while this information is absorbed. After half a minute or so, it is broken by me. 'I'm not sure that that's going to be fair to Donner and Blitzen and all the others, do you? One carrot between all those reindeer?'

'Well,' and now my wife's patience is just beginning to become a little strained. 'A lot of other people will have left a carrot for the reindeer, so no doubt Santa can make sure that they all get a fair share.'

The kids and I exchange glances. We aren't convinced, but probably this is the moment to let the subject go.

Lastly we have to pour a glass of sherry.

'Sweet or dry?'

'What?'

'Do you think Santa prefers sweet sherry or dry sherry? We've got sweet in case your Aunt Gloria comes, and dry in case your Aunt Audrey comes.'

By this time my wife is too preoccupied to have any interest in participating in my silly jokes. Because in the end I'm going to have to drink it and I detest dry sherry slightly less than I detest sweet sherry, Santa's going to get dry.

In those days we lived in a Victorian house with reasonably sized fireplaces, but they were certainly not large enough to admit a reasonably sized human being, let alone someone as lard-arsed as Santa. I sometimes wondered if the kids pondered such evident contradictions. On the one hand, naturally you don't want to raise the subject in case it hasn't occurred to them. On the other hand, you'd love to find a way to discover if your children are just a bit stupid.

Finally Lizzie and Matt placed their empty stockings on the floor, making certain they were in plain sight, and eventually, saucer-eyed and shattered, they'd be packed off to bed.

By this time I definitely want to go to bed as well, but as far as my wife is concerned, the preparations are only just beginning. Firstly, we have to wait up for an hour or more to ensure that the kids are settled in bed. Horror of horrors that they should come down for a glass of water and find the old man taking a crafty bite out of Santa's mince pie.

Then, when the coast is clear, we start planting the trail of evidence. I have to cut off all but the top end of the carrot, but then to bite the last bit so that Rudolph's teeth-marks can be cited in evidence. That's exactly what you need last thing at night on

Christmas Eve – a bite out of a carrot that's freezing cold because it's not long since out of the fridge; and with my teeth, too. Make a mental note to have a check-up first thing in the new year.

'Has Santa taken the carrot up to Rudolph, made him eat it, and brought the stump of the carrot back down again then?'

'Shut up.'

'OK.'

There is to be some consolation in being allowed to eat the mince pie, carefully leaving enough crumbs on the plate. A few large flakes, please, don't demolish the whole thing; and it is also my unwelcome duty to knock back the sherry, again leaving just enough in the bottom of the glass to tantalise the kids.

So now can we go to bed at last? Not likely. My wife has, of course, done most of the wrapping, but it turns out that she has made just a few last-minute purchases for the kids, and hasn't had a chance to wrap them. Oh joy.

To be fair, this is not something I've had a chance to check out widely among Grumpies of my acquaintance. However, my instincts are usually pretty good about this sort of thing. I suspect that more or less all of us absolutely bloody hate wrapping presents. Actually, now I do think about it, I guess we hate just about everything about presents, with the possible exception of receiving them, and even that is frequently a bit dubious.

Maybe it's because most of us are hopeless at it. The kitchen table is full of enough clutter to make Steptoe's yard look tidy, and so there is no surface big enough to lay out a whole sheet of wrapping paper. You could do it on the floor, but you're buggered if you are going to start crawling round on your hands and knees at this time of night.

Next you have to find the scissors and the Sellotape and take the object and work out what size piece of wrapping paper you have to cut up. In my case, if the thing I am trying to wrap is an irregular shape, and it usually seems to be, I'm stuffed. A box of Celebrations or something which, irritatingly, is bigger at one end than the other. Usually I'm pretty good at spatial awareness things, but in this instance I've got no idea. Chances are that I'll carefully cut out a shape which seems plenty big enough, but it'll turn out that the paper I've cut won't quite cover the box. Not quite. It leaves just about half an inch peeping through, thereby ruining any possible element of surprise. Worse still, the piece of wrapping paper that's left over is now also an irregular shape, and not quite big enough to go around anything. Or is it just me?

After half an hour of this, I'm feeling about as festive as Ian Duncan Smith on a works outing, and would willingly give any presents I'm due to receive to the homeless if I can only go to bed. But that's not quite yet.

There is still the vexed question of Santa's sooty footprints. Leave aside the fact that we haven't had a coal-fire in that room since Santa was a small boy, there has to be evidence of himself having walked around the living room arranging the various piles of presents. Not an easy one this – not without ruining the rug you just paid a fortune to have cleaned in the run-up to the holiday season.

Most years I think we settled for some mud from the bottom of a pair of size eleven Wellingtons. By the time we've finished, the whole place looks like a scene from the opening sequence of *CSI*. (I don't know how plausible you find it that a former stripper from Las Vegas could turn into a top forensic investigator, but I guess that stranger things must have happened. Probably.)

Anyway, back to the scene of the crime. Next the stockings have to be filled up with little parcels of this and that – their order carefully arranged so that there are some trivial things halfway down, but something worth waiting for at the toe. This usually includes the stuff that, when they were very young, they ended up playing with louder and longer than they'd play with their main presents. Maybe a puzzle where you had to rearrange little tiles with letters into a sequence. I used to spend hours on those myself. Or a little plastic paratrooper attached to some polythene that you could fold up and throw so it floated gradually to earth. Hours and hours of fun.

Or those little aeroplanes made of polystyrene cut-out pieces that you had to push out of a single sheet and put together. They'd glide alarmingly back and forth across the room until finally landing in the fireplace and causing a brief moment of panic as the flames from the festive log-effect gas-fire flared up the chimney. Anyway...

Two sets of presents are laid out, carefully arranged to ensure that both sides looked equal, with a line of tinsel separating them. Small fun things at the front, major presents at the back. Nothing left to chance.

And finally, when if we'd stayed up any later we'd stand a very good chance of meeting the real Santa on his early-morning rounds, my wife would sprinkle magic dust – little silver and golden moons and stars which Santa leaves in his wake as he arranges the presents round the floor. So how cool is that?

By the time she'd finished, I have to admit, the whole thing looked like something out of a Hollywood movie. The kind of scene you hope your kids will have etched on their memories as they leave the innocent world of childhood and enter the more cynical world of teenage... All is ready for that wonderful, most magical time... Christmas morning.

15

Christmas Morning

Well look, you've got to be more than an averagely miserable old sod to be grumpy about Christmas morning itself, but honestly.

It's well known that a high proportion of Grumpy Old Men suffer from insomnia. This can be caused by many things. In my case it can be something as trivial as having drunk too much wine, or equally I may inadvertently have drunk too little wine. I may have taken too much exercise too close to bedtime, or I may not have taken enough exercise during the course of the day. Going to bed too early can do it, as can going to bed after my usual hour. Eating too late is a good one, but going to bed hungry is another likely cause.

In other words, a lot of Grumpies have trouble getting off to sleep. Or maybe they get off to sleep quickly, and then wake up in the middle of the night. Or they wake up ridiculously early. None of which does much to underpin the earnest hope that they'll look and feel their best in the morning.

Then there is the question of the quality of sleep a Grumpy might enjoy when he's enjoying it. I, for example, go to sleep within about four seconds of my head hitting the pillow, and can easily have a deep sleep for anything up to three and a half hours before I start to become a nuisance to myself and anyone else in the house. I have been reported variously to have slept through the bathroom light going on and off, while various members of the family have come in and out to ransack the bedroom cupboards, and through thunderstorms out of classical mythology, sufficiently bright and loud to wake the Minotaur (who, I'm told, was a very deep sleeper).

For a few short and blissful hours I'm in a coma so deep that I'm in danger of being switched off, and then for no reason which I can identify, I'm awake. I'm awake, but dog-tired, irritable, too hot, restless, with my brain going at about 250 miles per hour.

This is all if things are going well. Like many Grumpies of my acquaintance, I can easily be plagued by horrible dreams which comprehensively spoil even these few short hours of relative bliss. If I make the stupid mistake of eating anything like cheese, Marmite, dark meat or any kind of crispy snack that's full of artificial flavouring, I'll usually have the sort of dreams that inspire horror movies, and which can easily involve me waking up with a jolt as I am pushed out of a twenty-sixth-floor window by Mark Thatcher or I'm stuck in a lift with John McCririck. Not a nice way to start the day.

Naturally, in common with almost every other Grumpy I know, during my brief comatose hours, apparently I snore. Loudly. Loudly enough, I'm told, to merit hiring in some consultancy from those very clever Japanese engineers who rebuilt Tokyo after the last earthquake. Loudly enough to penetrate into the most remote corners of hell and there to overwhelm the screams of the damned. Certainly loud enough to prevent anyone within a distance of several rooms of me from sleeping without earplugs or a pillow over their heads.

I, of course, deny that this can be quite as bad as is alleged, and my daughter Lizzie has often threatened to record it and play it back for me in the morning. So far, thankfully, that has not happened.

So again, like most Grumpies, I'm every bit as much of a joy to have around throughout the hours of darkness as I am during the day. And the only good thing about all this is that by the time I wake up – usually at about 2.30 or 3 a.m., my wife has taken her pillows and her eardrums into a spare room and I am alone. Which means I can listen to the radio. Which in turn means that I spend many hours absorbing a wide range of trivia from all around the world, thus providing a never-ending source of grumpiness, and with the retelling of which I can transfix everyone I meet during the following day.

Actually I just can't resist the temptation to pause here to give you an example from my insomniac monitorings of last night; and be assured that this is a true story. Somewhere in Bolivia or Peru, or somewhere else in South America, all of a sudden some blokes have been appearing in the streets, totally stark naked but smeared in mud. It seems that they are from a tribe that has lived a nomadic life in the rainforest and about which no one knew anything until about 1986. They've been in there minding their own business since before Cliff Richard first told us he was happy to be a bachelor boy until his dying day. Probably even longer.

It seems that these guys don't get the idea of property, and have been irritating the local drug warlords by wandering around and half-inching any of their stuff they can lay their hands on. So the warlords started killing them, and when they got fed up with that after a little while, drove them out of the forest and into the towns.

Anyway, the interesting thing about these blokes is that they're all walking around with monkeys sitting perched on their heads. 'That's unusual,' says the World Service interviewer. 'Are these pets?' There is a pause. The reporter doesn't know quite how to phrase his answer. Eventually he can think of no suitable euphemism. 'No,' he says carefully, 'they're lunch.'

It seems that these fellas eat monkeys, and while you and I have to stop at Upper Crust or maybe Pret a Manger if we're feeling rich and green, these blokes have found a way to enjoy something even fresher. How cool is that? And true. I heard it last night. Honest.

What all this adds up to is that the average Grumpy Old Man does not wake at seven in the morning and spring out of bed with a lightness of step which would be the envy of Wayne Sleep. Nor with a sunny outlook which would be the envy of Snow White. No, unfortunately, many of us wake up in the morning looking and feeling like shit. And, of course, spreading stardust and joy wherever we go.

John O'Farrell is a very funny man, and one of the things I like about him is that he is engagingly honest. Actually, I don't think he intends to be quite so frank when he sits down in front of our cameras, but something gets the better of him and he ends up giving far more revelatory glimpses into the real life of a Grumpy than maybe he planned.

For example, when I interviewed him for

the last series, I was amazed and delighted when he confessed that when he gets up in the morning, he's so stiff and wobbly and disorientated that he staggers to the bathroom and then has to sit down to take a piss. I thought this was an amazing revelation, delightful in its frankness, and I wondered if afterwards he would regret saying it. However when we were packing up the gear to go to the next location the sound recordist, a very fit bloke of about thirty, said, 'Yeah, I do that.' Then in the cutting room, the tape editor, who's a little bit older but cycles twenty miles a day, said, 'That's what I do.' And in post-production, the dubbing editor said, 'Yep, me too.' So did probably half a dozen other blokes along the way.

For me, part of the joy of the Grumpy Old Men experience is to discover that stuff you imagined you must be alone in thinking and doing is actually held in common with other Grumpies of your age or disposition. And I think a lot of Grumpies will find comfort in knowing that many other men of a certain age feel so horrible first thing in the morning that they cannot reliably stand up to wazzle. There you are – a public service if ever I heard one. Thank you John.

So, Grumpies, on Christmas morning like every other morning, there's a good chance that we're going to wake up feeling like a rat's bum, which is not a very good situation from which to get under way with what is supposed to be the most joyous day of the year.

I think there's something wrong with children if they don't start wanting to get up to see if Santa has been at any time from about 3 a.m. to 6 a.m. When Matt and Lizzie were small – before the cynicism and unattractive adolescent indolence of later years set in – we used to set an early limit of 6 a.m. And I have to admit that I, even I, used to find that their wide-eyed innocence and enthusiasm was such that it could break through the gloomy fog of dyspepsia that surrounds me when I first get up. My wife and I would confine them to their rooms while we went downstairs to switch the Christmas tree lights on, light some candles and do a last minute check on the evidence.

When all was finally arranged and in perfect order, we would go back upstairs, allow the kids to lead the way down again, tiptoe to the door of the living room, and at the word 'go' they would burst into the room, totally ignore anything to do with Santa's visit, and start ripping the paper off one present after another.

During this process my wife and I would occasionally say something naive like, 'Oh look, Rudolph has enjoyed his carrot' and one or both kids would glance up for just long enough to humour us before getting back to tearing off the shiny paper that some auntie had spent half an hour making look so lovely.

For the observant among us, there's a lot going on during these sessions, isn't there? The anticipation of Christmas has gone on for so long, and the preparations have been so extensive, that there is an unspoken but collective idea that everything has to be lovely. What that means is that, at some level or another, everyone present is in a way humouring everyone else. Do you know what I mean?

When our kids were little, we would gently direct them through the pile of presents. Obviously, we knew who everything was from, and in most cases we knew that Auntie June had sent socks again. So therefore we would carefully choreograph the order of openings to ensure that a couple of not very exciting items would be followed by a very exciting item, and then again maybe a less exciting item, with the ultimate objective that the climax would be at the end.

None of this is totally plain sailing for the kids either. When they're very young, they are totally spontaneous, and if something doesn't interest them, it is likely to be cast aside in an instant. Once they become obnoxious teenagers, they're not grateful for anything. But during those years in the middle – probably from about five to thirteen, they're playing along with the game just like the rest of us.

They know, for example, that it's not nice to be rude about the fact that Aunt Mimi hasn't noticed that it's some years since they stopped getting a kick out of jigsaw puzzles with twenty-four wooden pieces in the shape of animals. They also know that they have to pretend to be grateful for anything utilitarian which probably would have had to be bought at some time in the year anyway – like, for example, new pyjamas.

But it's a complex world, and so they're also having to keep an eye out for what their brother or sister is receiving, just to ensure that they themselves are not getting shortchanged. For instance, is a cowboy outfit complete with holster and a belt of silver bullets the equivalent of the make-up set, or not? Tricky. (And I know what you're thinking now – sexual stereotyping. Well, if you're thinking that, how do you know which kid got which present, clever dick?)

Anyway this calculation can be further complicated by an age range. Fortunately, Matt and Lizzie are close together in ages, but girls grow up quicker than boys, so there was a moment when she was getting 'my first CD player' or whatever it was, and he was still getting plastic monster robots that change themselves into vehicles, or something. Not an easy comparison to make, but the astute observer can see the calculations going on at lightning speed in little brain-boxes.

Most impressive of all, I think, is the way they manage to look grateful for almost anything, no matter how naff. A lurid pink 'My Little Pony lunchbox' from Auntie Kath, who isn't really an auntie but has been a friend of my wife's for so long that the kids think she is, doesn't know that Lizzie grew out of My Little Pony four years ago. A 'start your very own stamp collection' set for Matt from Uncle Tom. Regrettably Matt is about as likely to start his own stamp collection as I am to take up line-dancing, but to be fair to him, he makes a brief effort to look enthusiastic.

At last the moment arrives and they get to open their 'big presents'. The thing, whatever it is, that they've secretly been hoping against hope that they might receive, but dare not take for granted. Might they hope? Could it be possible?

One year in particular I recall they both desperately wanted new bikes, but my wife and I realised that there was no way to wrap them up that wouldn't make them obvious from the first moment that they nearly took the living-room door off its hinges as they burst through. We decided to just put a ribbon around the seats and leave them in the garage.

This led to a complex situation. When the

kids first perused their piles of presents, it was immediately obvious that there were no bikes among them. They realised that it was neither smart nor pleasant to lament visibly the absence of bikes, but yet it was plain as they opened the rest of their presents that there was an underlying disappointment.

At the end of the session of opening all the presents that were in evidence, their declarations of 'how lucky I've been' were, I seem to recall, pretty impressive. Only someone who knew them as well as we did would have been aware of the edge of disappointment. Naturally, when my wife and I started wondering out loud if there was any chance that Santa had been intending to leave anything but had not been able to bring it down the chimney, their joy became unconfined.

See what I mean? A lot going on.

Anyway, to return to the lot of the Grumpy. Traditionally it is at this point – after the kids, but before my wife – that I get to open my presents. Theoretically, out of everything that happens to a Grumpy in the twelve days of Christmas, or whatever it is, this is the oral-sex moment. This is the time for simply receiving pleasure, where the only obligation you are under is to find a way to express the appropriate level of appreciation. A succession of carefully calibrated responses to indicate that 'a little more of that sort of thing' might be welcome, or that 'that's very nice, but maybe not the very best thing'. So that the gift-giver will know what you're very pleased with, and also have the opportunity to take note for the future. An excellent metaphor, I think you might agree, but one which plainly I'm going to have to ditch well before the climax.

In my case I find this inordinately difficult. I've tried, God knows I've tried, but I find that my ability to express what seems or sounds like genuine appreciation for something I don't really want is reducing year on year. This may simply be because, as I am getting older and grumpier, it is harder and harder for anyone to buy me anything that I need or want. And that's probably because I'm too grumpy to need or want anything.

Even ten or fifteen years ago, I'd have a fair chance of receiving some books that I really wanted to read, or some music that I didn't have but had always wanted, or the odd shirt that would come in handy. Or maybe a desirable toy like a CD player or a Swiss Army knife. I didn't use to have much difficulty expressing pleasure and appreciation for stuff like this, and therefore the whole thing could pass off relatively painlessly for all concerned.

But how do you express sincere enthusiasm for a nice dressing gown 'because you've had your other one for twenty years'? How are you going to manage to seem pleased when you open a car-care kit with several varieties of polish, a novelty air-freshener and a mock chamois? I wear cuff-links about twice a year, so honestly I'm just not short of a little wooden box with a red felt lining to put them safely away in.

I mean, how are you going to deal with that? How can you be expected to manage to emit those little murmurings that say 'more, more'?

Whatever happened to the possibility of getting a drum kit for Christmas? When did I get too old to stand a chance of being given a saxophone? Or a really cool kite? I don't think I ever really wanted a black leather jacket with 'Satan' written in studs on the back, but what if I wanted one now?

The answer is, of course, that I'd be dubbed a sad old sod in his dotage, obviously having a mid-life crisis about ten years after his 'mid-life'. And that makes me grumpy.

Like it makes all Grumpy Old Men grumpy. And we're even more grumpy that we have to sit and look grateful to receive a load of stuff that's spookily similar to the sort of stuff which, as a ten-year-old, we used to sit and watch being given to our old grand-dad. And somewhere deep down in the memory we recall thinking how pointless it was to give him any presents, because there was so little time for him to use them between now and the grave. Now I'm that age myself, and I'm being patronised with exactly the same sort of stuff that we patronised him with, and I hate it. I fucking hate it.

So finally we get on to the last episode in the bizarre charade that is Christmas morning in the Grumpy household. The giving of presents to my wife. Presents that, because I am too miserable to go shopping and have no idea whatsoever what she might want, she has gone shopping for, she has selected, she has purchased and she has brought home.

A few years ago at least she would have given them to me on Christmas Eve so that I could make my pathetic efforts to wrap them up, etc. However, it seems that I must have been too difficult or miserable to do even that, because these days, come Christmas morning, she has even wrapped her own presents herself. And so now I have nothing to do other than hand them to her, without so much as a clue as to what they are. She even has to tell me in which order I should hand them over so that she'll open the more modest gifts at the start and the more exciting nearer the end.

And that's what it has come to. I guess it works. I guess it's very sensible. But it's not very festive, now is it?

16

'Tis the Season to be Bloated

We've wondered aloud in previous pages why it is that there are so many little rituals of one kind or another, which we all agree are totally preposterous and yet we all repeat, year after year after year. Other, of course, than that they provide endless material for Grumpy Old Men to complain about.

Christmas lunch is just one of those rituals.

Every year, without fail, we all cook and eat too much food for Christmas lunch. Every year we are going to eat a meal that has overflowed over the edges of our largest size dinner plates, we're going to be as full as a very full thing which has just been given an extra cow-pie to eat, and yet still we hear ourselves saying, 'Oh all right then, perhaps just a little bit more turkey.'

Every year we loosen our belts about midway through the meal, but still go on eating until we make ourselves so uncomfortable that all we can or want to do is to waddle over to the settee, flop down and go to sleep in front of the Queen. Every year we say some variation of 'never again', and every year we're going to do it again. It's a Christmas ritual, and we can't seem to stop ourselves.

The turkey is another thing. In our household we have turkey once a year. Once a year, and that's that for another year. Why? Because it is traditional. Forget that it tastes like blotting-paper dipped in cranberry sauce. It's basically very bland meat, and yet year in year out, for what is supposed to be the most important family meal of the year, we have turkey.

That said, I noticed a few years ago that some of our posher friends were not having turkey at Christmas. One or two were having a goose. I was so impressed by this that I started telling people that we were going to have a swan, and it's surprising how many people believed me. One or two even asked me where they could get one, so naturally I pointed them in the direction of the Harrods Food Hall. Then one or two others started having a 'nice piece of beef', and others even had a salmon. Weird or what?

However tempting these aberrations might be, over the years we've always stuck with turkey for Christmas lunch – partly because it is the traditional ritual, and partly because it's simple. Or at least it always was.

These days we're all used to our food becoming more and more poncey as time goes by. 'Rocket' where once we had 'cress', 'balsamic' where once we had 'Sarson's', 'free-range' this and 'organic' that. But is there any area, do you think, where this has reached more extreme levels of absolutely preposterous bloody absurdity than the Christmas turkey?

Last year, round about the end of November, my wife mentioned to me that 'We have to talk about the Christmas turkey'. I found this an odd notion. What could there be to talk about? Did she mean it in the same way that she used to say, 'We need to talk about Matt' when he had been caught smoking pot in the school cloakroom? I suspected not. Or even 'We have to talk about our holidays', in the sense that this year she was going to insist that we went on one? I genuinely had no idea.

'I was thinking about twenty-four pounds.'

I should say that it's become a running joke in our household that I always want a turkey about three times bigger than we could possibly need. When I say 'joke' I don't mean to imply that it's a side-splitter. It isn't. It's just another one of those little family foibles that we repeat year after year.

'Actually, there will only be the four of us, so I was thinking a maximum of 12lbs, but that's not what I meant.'

'Twenty-four pounds should be just about big enough then. What else did you mean?'

'Twelve pounds will be plenty big enough.

We need to discuss what kind of turkey we want.'

'Twelve pounds won't be anything like big enough. What do you mean ... "What kind of turkey we want"? We want one of those big feathery things with two legs, two wings and a neck like mine.'

Trying to curb her hilarity but also conspicuously not contradicting the last remark, she beckoned me over to the table to look at a twenty-page booklet from her favourite high street chain of stores, which seemed to be all about turkeys.

At this point I pause to say that I was going to mention the name of my wife's favourite high street store, and the reason I'm not is that they had been planning to order and stock huge quantities of the first book in the Grumpy canon – *Grumpy Old Men, The Official Handbook* – but when someone kindly pointed out to them that it was very rude about their totally depressing and soul-destroying clothes range (which incidentally I wear most of the time), they changed their minds. They'll get no mention in this book at all. Sit back and watch their share price plummet.

Anyhow, it was with some confusion and a slight sense of foreboding that I sat down to flick through this little booklet – and what a revelation it was. (Actually, if I'm honest, there wasn't really a lot of foreboding – we try not to do a lot of foreboding in our household – but I thought the idea might add a little drama to an otherwise fairly dull scene. Now I've written it, it seems silly, so forget I said it.)

All this may be familiar to you because you might have been forced to flick through this booklet yourself, in which case you are disqualified from participating in the following competition. But if all this is new to you, see if you can guess how many different variations of 'turkey for Christmas' you could buy in this nameless and soon to go bankrupt high street chain? If someone had asked me that cold, I'd have probably said two – one organic and one not. Maybe three at the outside – one born and raised without seeing sunlight, one free-range and one organic.

Well, obviously, you've got an advantage because of all this build-up, and you may be one of those bloody irritating people who says fifty-three in answer to a question like this. Anyway, let's struggle to the point. The answer is twelve. And the great joy is that none of them is just called straightforward, plain old 'turkey'.

There's 'oven-ready' which presumably means someone has plucked the feathers and stuck its innards in a plastic bag. There are three types of free-range and three more types of organic. There is something called 'turkey basters' – the busty amputees of the turkey world which consist only of breast-meat for people who don't like all the gnarly and sinewy bits you get with legs. There are turkeys that have been honey-dipped, turkeys that have been glazed with the extracted juice of Malaysian pineapples, and turkeys that have been massaged every day of their lives by Japanese peasants living at the base of Mount Fuji and have been offered a range of humane alternatives and eventually allowed to choose their own method of death.

Every sumptuous photograph is accompanied by a narrative which combines all the literary skills of the authors of an over-the-top travel brochure and an estate agent – including minute detail of the lifestyle, upbringing and academic attainment of said bird. And as you read every one of them you think, 'that sounds all right, we'll have that one' until you read the next one which also sounds all right, and therefore by the time you've read them all, you're totally confused.

Eventually I gave up and my wife made our selection, placed her order, and was given a rendezvous time on the day before Christmas Eve. Christmas Eve eve. Even then, she had to get up early to queue for an hour and a half to collect the thing at the appointed time, only then to stand and watch less prudent people who hadn't booked in advance come into the store, buy the turkey of their choice at the check-out, and be on their way

– all in the time it took her to move forward two places in her appointed queue.

When eventually we took custody of the turkey which was going to grace our Christmas lunch plates, I felt I knew it as well as I might have done if we had been adopting a child. It was a limited-edition black-feathered thing with a handsome pedigree. (I nearly said pedigree to die for, and I guess this is one of the rare occasions when that expression is accurate.)

And guess what? We compromised, as we more or less always do, on a fighting weight of about 16lbs, and our prized turkey ended up costing us just a wish-bone short of £65! – £65 for a turkey which used, about five minutes ago, it seems to me, to cost about £8. Can you bloody believe it?

In our TV programme about Christmas, Will Self asked the question why, if turkey is so delicious, we only ever eat it at this time of the year. Maybe we've just come up with at least a part of the answer; even people as gullible and downright stupid as we are prefer not to be mugged more than once every twelve months.

So that's the turkey, but that's only one aspect of Christmas lunch which is unique to that particular meal. When else, for example, do you cook carrots and swedes and mash them together to make a construction which, if it had a name, would probably be called something like 'neeps'? As a kid I used to assume that this was something we did in our household only because we'd run out of saucepans or gas-rings or whatever, but when we got married I discovered that my wife's family did it as well, and a straw poll among bored friends confirms that it's a familiar thing. It's not that they are particularly pleasant or otherwise together, it's just that it's a bit weird that we put them together at Christmas and at no other time. You don't think so? Well, maybe it's just me then.

And then you've got to have sprouts. Let's give everybody a pleasant surprise and make no jokes whatever about sprouts and their relationship to flatulence. It's not clever and it's not funny. No, the only thing you have to remember about sprouts is that you need to boil them for about eight minutes; which is easy enough most of the time, but when you're cooking Christmas lunch, there are about 1,000 things to do in the last ten minutes, and so the sprouts can easily be left cooking for longer than is optimal. In this case they take on the consistency of hot wet cotton wool and taste as vile as they did when you had them for school dinners, thereby identifying the reason why generations of children detest this much-abused vegetable.

We won't go through every item on your plate because it would take too long and anyway, who cares? Instead, let me tell you something which I think that any Grumpy Old Man reading this, or indeed his partner or children, might find surprising.

Every year, on Christmas Day, I cook lunch.

Yes yes I know, you're thinking that that explains why no one wants to come to our house at Christmas, etc. Very amusing, but essentially wrong.

Over the years we've had a variety of people to our house on Christmas Day, with a maximum catered for by me at any one time of thirteen. That included the kids, various in-laws, a grandparent or two and even, I seem to recall, an odd auntie. Some of our aunties are a bit odd, but this isn't the time to go into that. OK, so thirteen people for lunch; now maybe you're beginning to be a bit more impressed.

You may be confused by the question of how come a Grumpy Old Man – legendary for his lack of festive cheer and his ignorance and almost total indolence with regard to any other domestic activity – can or would step up to prepare Christmas lunch. Let me quash any doubts or misgivings immediately. It is an act of total selfishness.

A puzzle, you may be thinking. A contradiction. An enigma wrapped up in whatever it is. Anyway, the simple truth is that the credit you get for preparing Christmas lunch – one meal, once a year – totally outweighs the effort that's actually involved. It takes about six hours to do, on one day of the year, and you'll find that you get congratulated for it, on and off, for weeks and sometimes months before, and for weeks and sometimes months after. I doubt that there is any household activity where the ratio of work done to impressing people is so much in your favour. Which is why I strongly recommend it to other Grumpies.

The other thing is that, surprising as it may seem, cooking Christmas lunch is not that hard. There may be a lot of it, and there may be quite a few things going on at the same time, but Christmas lunch (certainly as I do it) is largely a question of timing and coordination. It's not like it's a major creation involving stews or reductions or flash-frying or whatever other technical terms proper cooks use. I don't do anything eccentric or stupid, like making my own bread sauce out of bread and sauce, or whatever the ingredients might be. I don't peel cranberries, or shell chestnuts to go in with the sprouts. Or is that walnuts? I've forgotten.

The way I do it, it's largely a matter of reading the labels on the packets, knowing how long it takes to parboil things like potatoes and parsnips before putting them in the oven, and backtiming everything from the moment when you want it all to happen. Not that hard.

And indeed this may be the right moment to put a pin into another balloon that I have stood by and watched being inflated over recent years – the idea that women are better than men at what these days we have come to call 'multi-tasking' – which is what I think at one time we used to call 'doing more than one thing at once'.

Like most Grumpy Old Men who have read the book or watched the *Grumpy Old Women* TV series, I have sat silently while Judith Holder does her excellent piss-take of her husband reading the newspaper and occasionally raising his legs to allow the vacuum cleaner underneath, while she is answering the phone, scrubbing the bath, cooking the meal, running a medium-sized multinational, keeping an eye on human rights, staying in touch with the relatives and educating the children. We've all laughed good-humouredly and raised our eyebrows. Probably we've even said something like, 'Yes, I s'pose you're right.'

But while all the time keeping our own counsel, privately Grumpy Old Men know that all that is bollocks. Obviously I don't know what you do, or did, for a living, but I run a little business that makes television programmes. Making television programmes involves having the ideas, doing the research, writing them up, seeing the commissioning editors, talking to the interviewees, writing the scripts, editing all the ingredients together, working with the narrator and putting the captions on. Just because it's fun doesn't mean that it's easy. What's the point of me telling you all this? The point is that when the chips are down, I can coordinate the timing of a lot of different stuff on gas-rings.

Actually, I find the only really challenging thing, apart from the fact that there are fewer gas-rings than items you want to cook and heat, is that last frantic five minutes. No matter how well organised you are, how coordinated everything is, there seems to be no way to avoid this last few minutes of dishing up becoming a panic.

At this point in the writing I should let you know that I've made a couple of attempts to narrate the sequence of events, but none of them has made the final edit because I can't seem to find a way to tell it without sounding like Nigella Lawson on acid. (A heady thought ...) So let's just say that there's a pan-demonium of carving turkey, draining vegetables, mixing those wretched carrots and swedes or whatever they are, scraping rather too-well-done potatoes and parsnips off the baking tray, extracting stuffing and/or sausage meat from unspeakable places, stirring gravy, bread sauce, and loads of other stuff I can't quite think of. And all this has to be done in minutes because there's nothing worse than a huge plateful of cold food.

Having achieved this culinary miracle, I am, of course, expecting everyone to tuck in quickly. So quickly in fact that no one will notice that the sprouts are cooked to a mush. However, this is to forget that there are several other ridiculous rituals which always have to go with Christmas lunch.

For some reason we have to have candles, and in our case we have a little ornament in which angels with trumpets have been cut out of very thin sheets of copper, and pirouette around in a circle trying to stop their private parts from being burned by the flames. We have to stop what we're doing and listen to the tinkling sound as they revolve. Very charming. Now can we get on and eat, please?

Nearly, but just before we do we have to pull the crackers.

Christmas crackers. I wonder if it's only the British that go in for all this indescribable bullshit. First, you have the conundrum of who is going to pull with whom. When my dad was alive, I was always so preoccupied that he should be included that I'd tell the kids to pull their crackers with him, and then my wife would pull her cracker with him, and then I'd pull my cracker with him. Poor old sod must have thought he was back in the trenches.

Then, just as you think it must be time to

tuck in to that succulent bird, it is announced that we have to put paper crowns on our heads, and any woman with a hair-do is thrown into a tizzy. I can never open mine without tearing it, and if I do it always tears when I try to get it over my oversized bonce.

OK. Good. Very amusing. I've got a large head. Now we're all sitting around looking like a parody of something out of Camelot, can we eat? Finally?

No, still not quite yet because now it's time for someone to start reading out the jokes. Is there a law, do you think, that prevents the inclusion in a cracker of a joke that is actually funny? Maybe it's an EU rule to prevent choking or something. Or to safeguard our shirts from the nasty bloodstains that would result from our sides splitting. On our *Grumpy Old Men at Christmas* TV spectacular, we allowed our cast of Grumpies to pull a festive cracker and to select some of their favourites. Well, you decide…

Will Self: What must you know to be an Auctioneer?

Lots!

Arthur Smith: 'I'm letting my pet pig sleep on my bed.'

'What about the smell?'

'He'll just have to get used to it.'

Jeremy Clarkson: 'Why do you call your dog "Metal Work"?

'Because every time he hears a knock he makes a bolt for the door.'

Rick Wakeman: What do you get hanging from Father Christmas' roof?

Tired arms.

John O'Farrell: What do you get if you cross a cowboy with an octopus? Billy the Squid. (John subsequently claimed to have written that particular joke.)

Rick Stein: Who is the most famous married woman in America? Mrs Sippi.

Rory McGrath: What did the beaver say to the tree? Nice gnawing you.

Ken Stott: How do you start a Polar Bear race? Say 'Ready, Teddy, go.'

Well, what did you expect?

OK, so now at last maybe we can start to eat – just a few mouthfuls anyway, before we're obliged to admire the pack of miniature playing cards or play with the tiny screwdriver set that has fallen out of the cracker. Oooh goody – the hours of fun we'll have with those later.

At this point, whenever I've been a guest at someone else's house in these circumstances, I always play the same game. You can try this at home. What you do is, you choose a moment of silence and then say something like, 'Lovely turkey, Mum.' And then sit back and wait. I guarantee that every single person round the table, one after the other, just a few seconds apart, will murmur some small variation on the theme.

'Moist' is one of my favourites. 'It's very moist,' which I assume is supposed to be a good thing. 'Very tender, Jean,' someone will say, 'where did you get it?' And then there will be a little discussion about the provenance of the bird. In the old days this used to be a brief history – nowadays, of course, thanks to people like the unmentionable high street chain, the story can take half an hour.

'Melts in the mouth' is usually a good one. Often followed by, 'Have you got enough dark meat there, Joe?' or whomever.

Go on; try it at home. I guarantee it. One after another, so that when it gets to the last person, they're bloody stumped for something different to say, and therefore might be reduced to, 'Yes, it's very tasty.' Well, you've got to get your fun where you can, haven't you?

Having made such a big song and dance about cooking the lunch, I have to admit that my efforts do come to an abrupt halt after what I'm pleased to call the entrée. I haven't a clue about dessert, always having taken the view that everyone is so stuffed by that time that there's hardly a corner left unstuffed in which to stow away anything else.

And anyway, how many people do you know who really like Christmas pudding? Maybe you're glancing through this book while the kids are playing with their 'see who can destroy the planet fastest and with most gratuitous violence' video-game, and your wife is trying to fathom the instructions on the new blender you've stupidly bought her for Christmas. If so, pause to take a show of hands. Who can honestly say that they like Christmas pudding? I'm guessing that either no hands will go up, or you're lucky enough to be a member of a family which is too polite to tell the truth about an annual ritual.

Here's my theory. Nobody actually likes Christmas pudding; if they did, it would be on the menu in restaurants and on the shelves at supermarkets all the year round.

No, Christmas pudding was invented as a joke somewhere sometime by someone who thought, 'What's the thing anyone would want to eat after they've already eaten the biggest meal they're going to eat in twelve months? Something light and fruity perhaps? Something refreshing that cleanses the palate? Maybe a little sorbet or at most something light and fluffy? No, let's give them a large wedge of something they could build a house with. Let's give them something that is so rich and heavy that if you had it as your first course instead of your last, you'd be pleading to be allowed to fast for a week before eating anything else. Oh, and because everyone will have so few other things to concern themselves with in the weeks leading up to Christmas, let's also make it take about a month to prepare and cook.'

And so they came up with Christmas pudding, and every year, just as with the Christmas turkey and the stewed-to-buggery sprouts and the mixture of carrots and swedes, we seem to have to get it down us. Because otherwise, how would we ensure that we felt like shit for the whole of the rest of Christmas afternoon?

17

The Box

As I think I've mentioned somewhere before, and difficult though you may find it to believe, I was at one time quite a big cheese at ITV. I'd worked there on and off for about twenty-five years, and when I left I signed an undertaking that I'd keep confidential any aspect of ITV's business that I had learned about in the course of my employment.

Actually, slightly to my own surprise, I've always respected this promise. But since this is a special occasion – it's Christmas after all

– I'm going to give everyone a little treat and let you all into a highly confidential commercial secret. And the reason I'm going to take this reckless course of action is not that I've suddenly developed a spirit of generosity towards lawyers and want to find them some work for early in the new year. No, rather it's because of an impulsive wish to provide an important public service by answering a question which I know for sure has been troubling the nation for as long as I can remember.

The question to which I refer is, of course: 'Why is the telly so crap at Christmas?'

I believe that for most people this genuinely is a conundrum. You'd think, wouldn't you, that seeing as the vast majority of people tend not to stray too far from their homes and their televisions at Christmas, it would be a fantastic opportunity for advertisers. You'd think that the chance to have a captive audience in the many many millions, all so overstuffed with Christmas lunch that they can't move a muscle anyway, would be too delicious to resist.

But it is not so, and indeed the key to the mystery is in that last sentence. There are plenty of us viewing the telly on Christmas Day – but we can't move. We're in slobbing-out mode, not in buying mode. If we should perchance see an advertisement for something we might want to go out and buy, we can't get up to go out of the house to buy it. Indeed, many of us can't even get out of the settee, let alone the house. And even if we did, the shops would be shut.

So even though there are unprecedented numbers of potential and actual TV viewers around Christmas, the advertisers by and large aren't interested in advertising to them. I said 'by and large' but there is, of course, one major exception, and you know what it is every bit as well as I do. Settees.

Anyone who has found themselves rejecting all the various types of drivel on the other channels over Christmas, and therefore reverted to ITV, will have been dumbfounded to see so many advertisements for settees. Or what is it that you call them? Sofas? Couches even? I never know. Whatever. It seems like there is one settee advertisement after the other. They're in white leather, they're in red leather, they're in leather the colour of shit. They turn round corners. They have little backrests which spring back and little footrests which spring out. They have obnoxious women draped all over them and even more obnoxious men, and let's not even start to talk about Linda bleeding Barker.

And the sale always start tomorrow.

So anyone who knows anything about the cost of advertising on the telly must wonder how it can be possible that there are so many people out there who want to go out

247

on Boxing Day and buy a new settee. And a settee the same colour as shit at that.

Maybe the answer is that you spend more time sitting on your existing settee over Christmas than at any other time of the year. You may well have been sitting there, picking at the loosening stitching on the arms and saying, 'We really must replace this old sofa' and then the advertisement comes on the telly and hey presto; that's solved the dilemma of how to spend a second day with the people you most love in the world. We can all take our minds off how much we hate each other by having a family outing to DFS.

But apart from settees and loads of discounted advertisements for the sales, no serious advertiser wants to spend any money on programmes over Christmas, and so the commercial channels don't want to spend much money on the programmes. That's that. Contract breached. I await the missive from m'learned friends.

However, what this brilliant analysis goes nowhere to explain is why the telly at Christmas is also mostly execrable on the BBC. They don't have any advertisers. They get their money through the licence fees extorted from people who are sitting down in their multimillions all over Christmas, desperate to have something to take their minds off Uncle Ernie's farting. Not that anything much short of Armageddon could do that, but we live in hope.

Every year since I can remember, someone has come home with the Christmas edition of the *Radio Times*, and we've sat down with a biro with the intention of drawing a circle around the things we'll make an effort to watch. Have you done this? I think so. When we were younger, and there were only four or five channels, the pages used to be covered in biro, with the rings overlapping irritatingly because something was always starting on BBC1 before the thing you were watching on Channel 4 had finished.

Maybe it's just that we've become harder to please, or maybe it's true that more channels really does mean there's less to watch, but in recent years the pages of the *Radio Times* have remained untouched. No matter how desperately or how frequently you scan those columns, there is simply bugger all that you really want to see.

There is a total of about twenty films which are trotted out in slightly different combinations year after year. If it's *The Sound of Music* this year, it'll be *Mary Poppins* next year. If it's *The Guns of Navarone* this year, it'll be *The Great Escape* next year. If it's *Chitty Chitty Bang Bang* this year, it'll be *Around the World in 80 Days* next year. If it's *Great Expectations* this year, it'll be *Oliver* next year. If it's ... well, you know them as well as I do.

And then there are the 'Specials'? This all started with the *Morecambe and Wise Christmas Special*.' By that I don't mean that Morecambe and Wise's was the first Christmas Special – far from it, but it's the one that became a national institution. Do you remember? The whole day used to be geared around it. Preparations for your cold turkey salad would be back-timed so that you could plonk down on the worn-out settee with a plate on your lap and the pickles and a glass of beer within handy reach, just as the opening titles would commence. The world used to stop for Eric and Ernie. It seemed as though everyone in Britain was watching, and I think they probably were.

Actually, if we're honest, I don't suppose they were as good as we remember them now, but what happened was that the enormous success of Eric and Ernie inevitably meant that every mediocre entertainment or drama in the schedules had to have its Christmas Special. And what are they like? Mostly, of course, they're a big disappointment. Either they're full of people who seem to be having a much better time than you are, so that you can see that this programme might have been fun to make but it's much less fun to watch. Or they're just self-indulgent bollocks. Usually I'm a big fan of Dawn French and Jennifer Saunders, but really?

Coronation Street will have to have a Special, of course. A few years ago ITV upset Buckingham Palace by starting an episode just before the Queen's Christmas broadcast so that the cast could appear to break off in the middle to watch her. That's nowhere near sensational enough these days, and the very least we require at Christmas now is a missing child, a serious illness or some domestic violence.

And because Christmas is a time for families, the usual run of ongoing domestic murders on *EastEnders* has to come to yet another climax of some sort. I've never actually watched an episode of *EastEnders*, but when it's on and you are totally bored you can have some childish fun by playing a game called 'Guess the next line'. What you do is to surf through the channels and go back to the show at a random point. You listen to one line of dialogue and try to guess the next one. You'll be amazed how often you can get it right – not least because seven times out of ten the next line is 'Leave it out, will ya? It's family.'

In fact I can think of only one example in recent memory of a Christmas Special version of a series which was really worthwhile – no, two maybe. Two out of dozens and dozens. *(Grumpy Old Men at Christmas. Grumpy Old Women at Christmas.)*

Channel 4 shows all the usual bollocks, or

251

a very slight variation of the usual bollocks. After all, it's Christmas, and because Channel 4 has to be a bit 'alternative', instead of showing the Queen they'll have a Christmas message from a gay person or whatever. Oh dear me, how very shocking. How very subversive. How very very dull.

And Channel 5? Well, what can I say? No doubt they are not designing their schedules with people like me in mind, but I honestly don't have the slightest clue what Channel 5 shows at Christmas. Do you? I guess it must be *CSI*. Every time I turn it on, it's showing *CSI*.

Christmas telly is shit, but then again, why wouldn't it be? Telly is shit at all times of the year; it's just that usually we've got alternative things to do. Christmas is the one time when you want to vegetate in front of it for hours and hours on end instead of doing something useful. And all this does for you at Christmas is remind you why you don't watch it for the rest of the year.

Like most people nowadays, we almost never watch anything on television at the time it's being broadcast. What we usually find is that one of our friends will tell us about a series they've enjoyed watching, but it's been on a channel we don't have or can't find, or more probably at a time I've already gone to bed. Anyway by now it is in the last few episodes of the run.

So being rather good at this sort of thing, my wife has usually stored up this information and bought some videos or (what is the latest way of making us buy the same thing again?) DVDs. This is when we catch up with what the rest of the world has been watching for the last twelve months. *House. Without a Trace. NYPD Blue. West Wing. The Sopranos. Six Feet Under.* All American, and all far, far better than anything we can produce in Britain. So just how depressing is that fact?

Sometimes over Christmas we'll sit there watching episode after episode, until the combination of too much food and too much wine overcomes me, and I'll wake up with a start several hours later, still on the settee, mouth lolling open endearingly, and dribbling down the front of my new T-shirt.

Sound familiar?

18

The Morning After

You probably won't have realised this and it's a little-understood fact – Grumpies prefer to suffer in silence.

I accept that this may be a bit difficult to

defend at the end of an entire book full of moaning, but what you may not be taking into account when rushing to your judgement of us as round-the-clock complainers is exactly how much suffering we go through *without* complaint.

For example, I haven't even mentioned until now the fact that for the last few days I've been in some considerable pain, and that as well as being responsible for cooking Christmas lunch, I spent part of yesterday morning – yes, Christmas morning itself – in Accident and Emergency.

OK, that's surprised you, hasn't it? You hadn't thought of me as long-suffering, now had you?

Well, since you ask, the story starts a couple of years ago when I made what turned out to be the terrible mistake of cutting a little nick into an apple tree, and rubbing some mistletoe into it. For some reason best known to myself, I thought it would be rather cool to be able to grow our own mistletoe. This turned out to be a mistake because the mistletoe flourished and is now in danger of ruining what had been a perfectly good apple tree. However, the point is that, five days before this Christmas, my wife asked me to cut some mistletoe from the tree so that we could hang a couple of sprigs above a doorway.

What a ridiculous notion that is. Though

the idea of kissing someone under the mistletoe gives you an initial frisson of excitement when you're young, the reality soon kicks in. I think I can honestly say that I never got to kiss anyone I fancied under mistletoe that I wouldn't have had a decent chance of kissing in a more intimate way later anyway. And anyone else I've kissed thus was always someone I wasn't especially interested in kissing.

Think about it. If you've genuinely got a memory of the mistletoe giving you an excuse to kiss the girl you always wanted to kiss, and she was so overcome by the potency of your kissing that she then became your concubine, that's a good story and I'm surprised. I think it's more likely that kissing under the mistletoe usually involved a fat cousin or a drunken aunt, than which there can be few worse fates.

So back to last week, and my little piece of amateur tree-surgery. I got out the Swiss Army knife which I love to own but so rarely have an actual use for, chose a blade from among the fifty-seven varieties, and began to saw. I know you're thinking that the knife slipped and I ended up gashing myself in that vulnerable fleshy part between thumb and index finger, but it was worse than that. Actually I don't know quite how it happened, but somehow I ended up with some mistletoe jammed underneath the nail of my thumb.

At the time it was unpleasant, later that day it was uncomfortable, the next day it was painful, and by the third day my thumb was the colour of a blood orange and the size and shape of an inverted Conference pear. By Christmas morning the pain was such that I had little choice but to repair to the A and E at Salisbury hospital.

Readers of the last book in the Grumpy canon will know that this was not my first trip to Casualty on Christmas morning. On Christmas morning fifteen years ago, and three months after the operation, I finally succumbed to the ongoing and searing pain following a vasectomy. As luck would have it, I ran into the surgeon who had performed the operation and had promised that any 'discomfort' would have passed after three weeks.

'What's the problem?' he asked.

'You said it would be three weeks, and I'm still in agony after three months.'

Any idea what he said? Would you like to guess? No? Well I promise you that these were his actual words: 'Well, you know how it is; three weeks, three months, who can be sure?'

I had to be physically restrained.

Anyway, for those of you who have never done it, I can recommend a visit to Casualty on Christmas morning. It may be the one moment in the entire year when it's quite quiet and there are a few staff working. Certainly you feel a bit of a prat sitting in Casualty with your thumb stuck up in the air, glowing like a Belisha beacon and throbbing like a throbbing thing. But, as it was Christmas, with goodwill to all men and all that, they even managed to appear fairly sympathetic.

'Mistletoe is very poisonous,' said the doctor. 'No no, you definitely don't want to get mistletoe into your system.'

'But since I have got it into my system, Doc, what are my chances of keeping my right hand?'

I assumed that he'd respond to this question in the same flippant tone that I had posed it, but his face didn't flicker: 'Oh I'd say about 50/50,' he said, and reached for his scalpel.

OK, so I'm telling this story now to make the point that I suffered in silence all Christmas Day. Hell, I even told the whole saga about cooking lunch without mentioning the added handicap of a massive bandage round my thumb and the excruciating pain. So there; suffering in silence, for which I received precious little sympathy.

And the other reason for telling this story now is that terrible pain in a blood-engorged thumb nicely sets the scene for what happened on Boxing Day. But just before we get to that, here's another surprise for anyone who expects Grumpy Old Men to be irredeemably grumpy about every aspect of life in general and Christmas in particular.

Boxing Day is, I think, my favourite day of the year. Potentially.

Well, think about it. By and large, all the bollocks of Christmas is more or less over for another eleven months. You don't have to worry about whether the presents you're giving are going to be welcomed, or how you're going to manage to look grateful for presents you will be receiving but are not going to want. That's in the past, and by the time Boxing Day comes around, either you've managed it, or you haven't.

Most of the people you don't really want to see have come and gone, and all of the bloody trauma and tension surrounding buying, cooking and serving Christmas food is over. Sure, you feel like shit from having eaten and drunk enough for four people and their horses yesterday, but as you've nothing to do but to slob out, it's not the end of the world.

With all the excitement and having had only about four hours of sleep in the previous twenty-four, the kids are shattered and likely to wake up late. When they do, there's a decent chance that they'll be reasonably subdued and fairly absorbed in some obnoxious video-game in which the Titans of Omnivore have to brutalise and master the virginal maidens of Abroxxa. Or something equally vile. And it's one of the very few days of the year when you don't really feel obliged to ask them some variation of 'Shouldn't you be doing homework/reading a book/studying for your exam?'

All that is if the kids are under fifteen, of course. If they're over fifteen, they probably went out last night 'with me mates' and if they came home at all, got back so late that you probably won't see them until 4 p.m. Bliss.

So one way or another, everything should be set for a Grumpy to have a really nice day.

Left to myself, a perfect day for me is one in which I don't actually ever get out of my dressing gown; and this is especially attractive on Boxing Day because the volume of rubbishy food that was disposed of on the previous day means that anything involving a belt is likely to be unwelcome. In and among all the impertinent rubbish, I might have received one or two books I'd quite like to read, and despite what I said before, I may even have got some music I'd quite like to listen to. In short, it may be the only day of the year when there is absolutely no reason on earth why I can't totally – what's the expression that Matt and Lizzie use and which irritates me so much? – oh yes, it's 'chill'. That's a perfect Boxing Day.

Of course, it is the lot of Grumpy Old Men that no legitimate wish of ours can be allowed to run its course, and there is always some fuckwit somewhere who seems determined to urinate in our lemonade.

This year just gone, I was all set. My plan was to stay in bed late and start on one of the several mindless paperbacks I'd received. And that's another thing: I once read a trashy detective novel by Patricia Cornwell about a forensic scientist called Kay Scarpetta, and made what turned out to be the elementary mistake of saying out loud that, rather to my own surprise, I'd actually enjoyed it. Because I'm so difficult to buy for, every year from that year to this I've received whatever is her latest. Unfortunately, none of them has been anywhere near as good as the first one. Don't you find that all the time?

Anyway, despite recent disappointments, I was looking forward to starting this one and, in this hypothetical perfect day, my plan was to read for a while, then get up at around 8 a.m. and make a bacon sandwich. I'd bring it back to bed with a cup of tea and read some more. Eventually I would get up again, loaf about, watch episode 4 of the latest batch of *Six Feet Under*, and then loaf about a little bit more.

Around about twelve I'm likely to start feeling a bit peckish, and here's the key to my penchant for turkeys twice the size of anything that could ordinarily be justified. I like turkey cold in a brown-bread sandwich, ideally with a bit of stuffing and some cranberry sauce. The most important decision you want to have to make on a day like this is Branston or Piccalilli.

All sounds as though it's shaping up nicely, doesn't it?

The warning that things might not work out exactly as planned came with the sound of the phone trilling at half past nine in the morning. Do you find that sound itself persecuting? I do. The phone used to ring; you know, like with a bell. It was neither particularly pleasant nor unpleasant, but it alerted you to answer it. Nowadays there are about 480 variations of music, vibration or trilling, and all of them go right through you like a knife. I actually get a knot in my stomach if someone's mobile rings as a sound-effect in *The Archers.* So at a moment like this, when you're looking forward with innocent naivety to the perfect uninterrupted day, it's about as welcome a sound as the new single by Liberty X.

Left to myself, I wouldn't answer the phone, but my wife always thinks someone has been taken ill or something, so she picked it up. And what is amazing is how, after you've lived with someone for a while, you can tell so much merely by the tone of voice in which they're saying 'uh-huh'.

In this case it was a series of 'uh-huhs' which the person on the other end of the call would have taken as acquiescence, and which I could tell at ten feet away actually indicated dismay. Even worse, I could tell from these two short syllables that my wife was having to agree to something that she knew would go down with me like a sharp-edged ice-cube up the rectum. (For clarification, and in the unlikely event that there are any weirdos out there reading this, I do mean badly.)

Well, this turned out to be my ordeal, not yours, so I won't visit on you a blow-by-blow account. Suffice it to say that Judy and Alan were on their way from their home in Cardiff to catch the cross-Channel ferry, and because someone somewhere was on their annual strike, their booking had been cancelled. As luck would have it, they had a few hours to spare and were not far away. So as they had nothing to do for some hours, and happened to be in the neighbourhood, they wondered if this might be a convenient moment?

The series of 'uh-huhs' from my wife continued for about five minutes and I knew that disaster loomed when she finished with the words, 'Oh, so you're just coming off the motorway now? So about twenty minutes then? No no, that will be fine. No, we'd love to see you.'

She replaced the receiver and looked at me. I looked back at her. We looked at each other for a long time.

'Don't tell me.'

She told me.

'I just don't fucking believe it.'

'I know, I know, but what could I say? It's Boxing Day. Where else could they go?'

Don't you hate it when you start saying stuff that is totally unreasonable, and which you know is totally unreasonable, but you just can't stop yourself? That's what I started doing. 'They could go to bloody hell, that's where they could go. You could have told them we were going out, or that we were expecting a visit from some friends with leprosy, or that we had all contracted the Black Death and that the Grim Reaper was calling at any moment.'

'Or that I'm married to a totally selfish and miserable bastard who hates seeing anyone at anytime, even over Christmas which is supposed to be a time for goodwill to all men?'

'Exactly! Precisely! It's not too late. Let's get them back on the phone and tell them the truth!'

Well, of course, we didn't, and sure enough Judy and Alan, and their little darlings Petra and Winky and Triffid, or whatever the hell they were called, duly landed about ten minutes later while I was still in the shower.

To complete the bliss, their kids were also just that bit too young for our kids to be anything other than irritated by them. Mark and Lizzie were not thrilled to see a plastic model of Petra's latest character from Harry Potter or whoever it was, and for once I didn't blame them.

So there it is; the one bright shiny jewel in what is otherwise the ocean of mud that is Christmas trampled underfoot with a size nine hobnail, and any chance of a bit of total indolence last seen disappearing into the mists of lost hope. A bit dramatic? Well maybe, but for goodness' sake.

That was it. The Addams family succumbed to my wife's entreaties to stay for some cold cuts and eventually left at about three o'clock. I spent what was left of the afternoon eating an unwise number of chocolate Brazils, watched a few DVDs and went to bed feeling like I'd been inflated. So that was Boxing Day for another year.

Isn't life wonderful?

19

Consumer-mas

So that's more or less it then, is it? Christmas for a Grumpy. The culmination of weeks of old bollocks, crammed into two days of claustrophobia and overindulgence. And as with so much else in the life of a Grumpy Old Man, you are left wondering what it was all about.

What *is* it all about? Certainly we can agree that Christmas is a celebration. All that beer and wine, all those sausages on sticks, crackers, party-poppers (not that kind); it all adds up to a celebration of sorts. Where we might begin to differ, just a bit, is over the question 'Of quite what?'

Obviously, we don't want to offend anyone (by accident), so we should say straight away that for many it's the celebration of the birth of Jesus Christ. Remember? Born in a manger. No room at the inn, all that good stuff.

But let's be honest, the celebration of Christmas for most of us in Britain has nothing whatsoever to do with all that; and indeed it's one of the several hugely en-

265

dearing things about the British that we are now probably the most secular nation on earth, with belief in Christ retreating faster than a politician being held to a promise, yet there's no sign at all of any reduction of interest in the holiday which marks the central tenet of the faith.

But if in reality it's not a celebration of the birth of our saviour, what is it a celebration of?

As we said somewhere near the start, for Grumpy Old Men there's something to be said for celebrating coming to the end of another crap year and still being alive. When you get towards the latter end of your grumpy years, you do begin to feel grateful to have made it through another one. Chances are that in the last twelve months a couple of people you knew quite well have died, a couple more have contracted something horrible, and a couple more have wives who have finally decided that life doesn't have to be this way and have buggered off to find out what it could be like.

So if, as a Grumpy, you get to the end of another year and all your moving parts are more or less working, and no one very close to you has departed, maybe that's a reason for celebration. A sort of extended 'phew'.

But all that's for Grumpies and older. When you're young, you believe you are bloody superman – invulnerable and immortal. Just surviving intact to the end of another year is something you entirely take for granted. So if you are a young and relatively healthy heathen bastard, what then are you really celebrating on 25 December?

Let's cut to the chase and face up to it, shall we? It's a celebration of buying and having things. It's a festival of covetousness, envy and greed. Christmas is a celebration of Consumerism.

It's the time when every provider of every service, and every manufacturer of every consumer product, gets their rocks off. From sweaters to sweets, from laptops to lap-dancers, and from Snickers to knickers. No matter what sort of business you're in, if you've had a crap year, there's always the chance that Christmas will bail you out, and usually it does.

Think about it for a moment. What do the manufacturers of advocaat do for the rest of the year? When else but at Christmas would anyone be interested in buying a bottle of yellow-coloured phlegm? I can only imagine that these, people take eleven months of the year off, and then come to work around October. They spend about a month mixing as many eggs with as much snot as they can gather, put it into bottles, and then take the rest of the year off. All so that when Auntie Margery pops over on Boxing Day we can say, 'Would you like a snowball, Margery?'

and she can say, 'Oh well, as it's Christmas.'

Or what about 'Eat Me' dates? What is that all about? Has anyone ever seen or heard of an 'Eat Me' date at any time other than Christmas? Of course you haven't. But somehow or other, as regular as the arrival of traffic wardens at 8.30 in the morning, they appear in the shops in early December. And we buy them? Why? Well, just in case someone might get peckish in the forty-five-minute interval between the end of lunch and someone asking if you'd like a cold turkey sandwich.

And who eats crystallised fruit at any other time of the year than Christmas? Do you know anybody? Of course you don't. And how has the ever-vigilant EU allowed these people to continue to write the word 'fruit' on the outside of a box of crystallised fruit? The people that won't let you call it Parma ham unless it comes from Parma, or a sausage unless it's the shape of a sausage or whatever. What relationship do the contents of a box of crystallised fruit have with fruit? Eh?

OK, so I'm off on one, and we need to get back to the point. Christmas is the time for every manufacturer of every product to bust a gut to reach their annual sales targets. That's how a 'good Christmas' is measured in Britain today. You don't think so? Think about it.

How many times, in the six weeks before Christmas and the few days after it, will you hear headlines on the news spouting some variation of 'High street retailers say it's a good/bad/exceptional Christmas'? There then follows some grim-faced reporter telling us that shoppers are 'waiting for the sales' or 'being careful', or 'spending like a drunken sailor' or whatever. Earnest-looking store managers talk about the level of spending in terms and in tones more suited to coverage of the tsunami.

Of course they do. They're not measuring Christmas on the basis of how spiritual we all are, or on how many of us went to church, or how many of us volunteered to feed the homeless. It's not being measured on how many conflicts around the world were resolved, or how much was received by charities. How much peace and goodwill to all men. Certainly not how many people raised a glass to the birth of Jesus.

No, no. It's being measured by how much we spent. It was a 'good' Christmas if all the shops did well and we all consumed obscene amounts of food, drink and associated junk. We all spent vast sums of money on presents we could ill afford and which no one really needed or wanted. It was a 'bad' Christmas if anyone, anywhere did anything in moderation.

Will Self suggests that we should rename

Christmas 'Consumer-mas' and he's right. Christmas is a celebration of obscene levels of consumption, so that all of us get to start the new year overindulged, overfed, overweight and needing to work overtime to pay for it all.

So that's Christmas for another year then, and thank God that Grumpy Old Men can now give everyone else a rest, stop moaning on about it for another twelve months, and safely return to the more routine levels of grumpiness that pervade the whole of the rest of the calendar.

Now wash your hands, please.

The publishers hope that this book has given you enjoyable reading. Large Print Books are especially designed to be as easy to see and hold as possible. If you wish a complete list of our books please ask at your local library or write directly to:

Dales Large Print Books
Magna House, Long Preston,
Skipton, North Yorkshire.
BD23 4ND

This Large Print Book, for people
who cannot read normal print,
is published under the auspices of

THE ULVERSCROFT FOUNDATION